STONE DEEP

A STONE COLD THRILLER

J. D. WESTON

STONE DEEP

CHAPTER ONE

The Defeat of the Floating Batteries at
Gibraltar commanded the opulent gallery;
even Cordero Diaz thought so, whose knowledge of the fine arts could be written long-
hand on the rear of a cigarette packet.

The painting was more than just a scene
painted on a canvas. The brush strokes, visible in the texture of the oils, had purpose.
They were not the simple result of applying
colour to creation using a brush as a medium.
Instead, the strokes conveyed tones, shadows
and direction, and complemented neighbouring colours, tones and shadows. The
depth of the foreground, with its hues of
green and deep shadow, was not there to fill a

gap between the background and the content. The foreground had lines that drew the viewer's eye to the life of the art, its heart and soul. Soldiers on horseback were described in so much detail that a modern photograph could not portray the scene with more clarity. A washed blend of pastel colours, used to invoke a terrifying scene of battle, anguish and carnage, invoked the smell of gunpowder to the viewer, along with fire, smoke, and death.

The painting was a masterpiece.

At close to seven metres by five metres, removing the frame from its position of glory five metres high on the wall of the gallery would require planning. But it was not impossible. If it was possible for one man to create such a masterpiece, it would be possible for a team of men to steal it.

Falling in with a guide and a host of tourists, Cordero played the part of an inquisitive visitor well; this wasn't his first rodeo. He knew the rules of engagement. Invisibility was key.

The remainder of the tour, although interesting, was spent examining security, adding more research to what the team had already discovered through their planted security guard. Lasers did not protect the Guildhall Gallery in the City of London. A web of infra-red beams was not switched on when the doors were locked, ready to sound the alarms should an inexperienced intruder fall foul of their purpose. But behind the walls and beneath the raised floors was a mesh of sensors. They all connected to the control room in the basement, where a team of guards monitored them around the clock.

Cordero noted the camera positions, and with a series of timely nods from one of the planted guards standing nearby, he managed to photograph the security challenges they might face under the guise of artistic interest.

"Erm, excuse me," said the guide, as Cordero leaned over the barrier to photograph a Monet in the corner of the room beneath a security camera. "There is no photography allowed. Did you see the signs?"

Cordero stepped back from the painting.

"No entiendo. Lo siento," he replied.

"No está permitido," said the guide.

"Ah," said Cordero, feigning a sudden understanding. "Sí, lo siento."

He finished with an embarrassed smile as the eyes of the tourists all returned to the guide, who continued to explain how German bombers destroyed the gallery during the blitz of World War Two. He described how many of the paintings that were displayed had been temporarily removed and sent for safe keeping just three weeks before a lucky hit from a Nazi pilot destroyed the gallery. Cordero ignored the speech, aware of the gallery's history. Instead, he memorised the brand of the security camera. It was a detail that his photo would have captured, and would allow his tech guys to plan the security breach.

The tour took another forty minutes to complete, during which Cordero noted several paintings that would be far easier to remove and steal, and were likely worth a great deal more, black market or not. But Dante had specified The Defeat of the Floating Batteries at Gibraltar, claiming it to be a lifetime ambition to own the masterpiece, and because of his ambitious nature, the logistics of the operation were minor details. If Cordero knew Dante as well as he thought he did, it would not be long before the painting would be installed in Dante's house, although he couldn't think where it would go. A painting of such magnitude would require a room with walls far greater and grander than Dante possessed.

As the guide completed the tour and answered the final question from an Asian tourist, Cordero loitered for the opportunity to thank the guide in his best broken English, and to apologise for his lack of thought, stating that he became overwhelmed with admiration for the painting.

"It happens every day," said the smiling guide. "I hope you enjoyed the tour?"

"Ah, sí," said Cordero, in an attempt to sound enthused. "Perfecto."

The guide opened the door to the staff-only room, and offered Cordero a "Ciao," as he stepped away.

Cordero took a final glance up the sweeping staircase into the gallery, catching a final glimpse of the target, then turned to leave.

The walk from the gallery to Liverpool Street Station took just five minutes, and the train to the leafy London suburb of Brentwood was waiting at platform eight. Cordero chose an empty carriage. But three schoolgirls, who appeared to be skipping school, joined him and took a booth a few seats away, laughing at nothing while playing music through the loudspeaker on one of their phones. The girls disembarked at Stratford Station where a man entered and selected a seat at the far end of the carriage.

Cordero searched through the images he'd taken before the guide had caught him snapping photos. He sent them to Diego as instructed. Diego would ensure the team received the images. By the time Cordero arrived back at the garage, plans would already be in motion.

As the train approached Brentwood, Cordero waited by the doors. The man at the far end of the carriage, who was of slight build and engrossed in his phone, ignored him. A lady at the other end of the carriage, who Cordero had not noticed, collected her bag and was standing beside the doors closest to her seat. She checked her watch and peered out of the window. Perhaps she was checking for her husband who would collect her. Or maybe it was a lover? Cordero could smell her perfume; it was rich, not floral, but light with a hint of sandalwood and fruit. She unfastened the top button of her blouse. Cordero smiled to himself and pictured her steamy clandestine meeting with her infatuate. Perhaps she would allow her hands to wander as he drove them to his house. Perhaps she would offer a glimpse of whatever lay beneath the small skirt she wore; a tease before the delights of their taboo relationship unfolded.

Cordero followed the woman from the train, down the concrete steps and through the barriers, which had been left open during the day until rush hour, in a move to reduce the manpower needed to manage the station. He slowed his walk and admired the view of her behind, hoping to glimpse whatever the lucky man would be enjoying over the next few hours with her.

The station was empty. The street outside appeared quiet. The woman turned left.

Cordero followed.

She walked thirty metres from the station entrance then, with a practised casual manner, she glanced back once and slipped into the passenger side of a waiting SUV. Cordero slowed then stopped and made to cross the road. He turned his head to check for traffic as the first blow connected with his throat, crushing his windpipe. With wide panicked eyes, he turned to face the attacker but found nobody.

Cordero gasped for air. He leaned on a post to support himself. Then, from nowhere, his chest felt like it had been hit with a hammer and the static sound of a taser sang like a warning bell as fifty thousand volts raced through his body, stunning his senses. The taser stopped. Cordero reeled from the blast of energy as someone pulled a thick bag over his head. He fought to remove it and lashed out at the attacker, but a hard blow to his gut sucked the wind from him. A second blow, which slammed into his temple, rocked his vision and turned his world from a dizzied array of spinning lights to the peaceful, pitch dark of unconsciousness.

CHAPTER TWO

"Do you remember I asked for your help, Lola dear?" asked Smokey.

"I do," Lola replied, "and can I presume that you have some kind of masterplan and the garage has something to do with it?"

"You'll see," her father replied, and squeezed her hand.

Samuel, Smokey's driver, pulled the sleek Mercedes minivan up to the doors of Smokey's brand new garage, which had been built in a thicket of trees on the far side of the lake at the south end of his vast property. Lola slid the side door open, stepped out, and waited for Samuel to slide the two stainless steel ramps into place, so she could then wheel her father down into his workshop.

"I could walk if you'd help me, Lola," said Smokey from inside the van.

"You heard what Doctor Fenn said, Dad," she replied. "You need to keep the leg elevated and rested to heal."

"Yes, well, he that can't endure the bad won't live to see the good, Lola."

Samuel gave her the nod, and helped her guide the wheelchair to the ramp. She stepped up, tilted it back, and lowered her father to the ground.

"I hate all this," her father complained in his thick London accent.

Lola pushed the chair past Samuel, leaving him to remove the ramps and park the minivan. She pushed the chair into the garage, which was a brick-built rectangle with a forty-foot-high ceiling and electric rolling shutter doors. The garage was a new addition to the property and contained Smokey's collection of beloved vintage cars.

"Well," said Lola, "are you going to tell me what this is about?"

"Lola, sweetheart, before we go inside, I have to tell you something."

Lola recognised her father's tone.

"What have you done?"

"Not me. Well not directly."

"Just tell me," she said.

"I had to get some outside help."

"So? What type of help?"

"I needed..." He hesitated. "There's no easy way to say it, so I shall just say it. I needed somebody kidnapped."

"Kidnapped?" said Lola, then checked her voice. "What on earth?" She craned her neck to see through the door.

"He is exactly who we have been looking for," her father replied. "Now we have him, we will extract the information. It's important, dear. Please, you must understand."

Once inside the garage and on the smooth, painted screed floor, her father wheeled himself, preferring to maintain his independence as much as possible. Lola walked beside the chair as they approached the far end of the large room.

A man lay on his back on the floor. Tied to each of his limbs were thick lengths of manila rope. Each hung in long, sweeping curves over four separate roof beams and collated near a pulley in the ceiling space, which ran through a series of other pulleys. A single length of manila rope hung on the far side of the room, and the manner in which the man was tied meant that a tug on the single rope would lift him from the floor and stretch him apart.

Lola's father stopped his chair at a safe distance from the man, but close enough to see his panicked face. Lola took her place beside him.

"So, you're awake now. You must be Cordero?" said Smokey.

Cordero remained silent but continued to search around him, as if some beast lurked out of sight.

"Do you know who I am, Cordero?"

The man let his head fall back, overcome by his struggles.

"Do I look like I care who you are?" he replied. His Spanish accent was thick.

"Now, now, pleasantries will get you everywhere, my boy. We'll have no more of that."

"What is it you want?" Cordero asked. "I know nothing. I don't know where I am. I don't know who you are. And I don't know what you want. You want to kill me? Just kill me. You want to let me go? Just let me go. But do not sit there and ask me these idiot questions."

"My name, my ill-mannered friend, is Smokey the Jew. But you can call me Smokey. Perhaps you've heard of me?"

"Smokey the what?"

"Smokey the Jew. It's quite simple."

"No, I have never heard the name. I don't care who you are, just tell me what you want. All these stupid games..." His voice trailed off into a rant of heavy Spanish.

"You're in an unfortunate position, and for that, you have your boss to thank. Sadly I don't think you'll get the chance."

Cordero pulled on his restraints, more out of frustration than a genuine effort to escape.

"Dad, are you sure-"

Her father turned to her, his brow furrowed. Lola stopped mid-sentence.

"Lola, can you leave us please?" he asked.

"But, Dad-"

"No buts, ifs or maybes, Lola. Leave the room. Prepare for a small operation. Just as soon as Cordero talks."

"How will you get-"

"I'll call Samuel. I'll be okay. Now leave."

Lola stepped away from her father and took a slow walk back to the door where she stopped, turned, and watched as Smokey wheeled himself closer to Cordero. He spoke softly with genuine compassion.

"I feel I should take the opportunity to warn you, Cordero," he began, "of the lengths I will go to stop your boss' plans."

"You think he will care that you have me?" replied Cordero. "You think that somehow you have now the upper hand?" His laughter seemed to hang in the open space, then died as abruptly as it was spat.

"No, I don't. In fact, I don't think there is one person alive that will miss you. Am I right, Cordero?"

Cordero remained silent.

"I presume by your silence that I am right?" said Smokey.

Lola slunk down out of sight of her father, but with a clear view of Cordero.

Cordero responded once more with silence.

"But you will suffer. Brutality is not in my nature, you know? Oh no. It never has been, and I didn't get where I am by dishing out penance to others. I'm not a violent man, but sometimes, Cordero, sometimes the greed and evil that overcomes others just needs to be stopped. And do you know what I think to myself, Cordero?"

"I don't care what you think. You are insane."

"I think, what is all this wealth? What are all these possessions? And what is this power if I can't use it to bring a little good back into the world? Because, and this is something I truly believe, the world is a good place, Cordero, full of good people. But sometimes they're led astray, as was Judas Iscariot. He wasn't a bad man. He simply fell foul to human nature. So with all this power and wealth, Cordero, I'm able to steer a select few of the misguided onto the right path. The path of righteousness, as it's so often called."

Cordero groaned as his own weight took its toll on his arms and legs.

"What is it you want?" asked Cordero.

"Your boss has veered from the path of righteousness, Cordero. He has taken a path lined with gold and wealth, but sadly, that path leads to nowhere but hell." Lola's father spoke slowly and articulately. "And with your help, I intend to steer him back onto the path of righteousness."

Smokey looked up to the end of the room. His eyes conveyed a silent command.

Lola glimpsed movement from the shadows of a small room at the far end of the garage.

An upright beam blocked her view, but she was sitting on her haunches, waiting for whoever it was to step into sight. A black jacket, dark jeans and heavy black boots were all Lola could see.

"This is your last chance, Cordero," said Smokey. "Your last chance at dying a quick and easy death."

Once more, Cordero's snappy bark of a laugh reverberated around the room.

"Then I'm afraid you have chosen a path that even I can no longer help," replied Smokey. "You will now suffer. How much, I do not know. But my friend here is highly skilled. He will keep you alive when you hang on the brink of death, and he will reel you back for more. You will tell me what Dante is planning, Cordero, one way or another. How much pain you endure before you do so, well, that's your choice."

Smokey turned to the figure in black, and even from the distance that Lola was spying on them, she caught the slight nod of her father's head.

Lola gasped when the figure stepped from the shadows. Framed in the light of the rear window with an almost childish look of intrigue etched on his face may as well have been death himself.

"Harvey Stone," she whispered.

Harvey stepped up to Cordero, took a deep breath, and then began.

Her father no longer acknowledged Harvey, as if by doing so, he removed himself from the imminent atrocities. Harvey required no acknowledgement. His presence filled the room. Lola kneeled, transfixed, at the door and watched as the man who had saved her life only a few months before, so brutal and yet so righteous, took hold of the rope and worked the pulley system. Cordero hung from his limbs rising six inches at a time, powerless to defend himself. He protested; loud, harsh Spanish insults flew from his mouth in rapid bursts until he hung six feet in the air. Then he silenced.

Lola's father also waited in silence until

Harvey had stopped, tied the rope off and reached for five heavy sandbags that hung on the walls from large S-shaped butcher hooks. He carried three in one hand and two in the other, stepped over to Cordero and dropped the three at his feet. He then switched the sandbags to his other hand, positioned himself between Cordero's legs, and lifted the two hooks above Cordero's knees.

Cordero was shaking. He raised his head and peered down the length of his body at the two razor-sharp hooks and heavy sandbags. Then he uttered a reel of Spanish as the reality of what was about to happen hit him.

"Tell me the plan, Cordero," said Harvey, and he let the sharp points of the hooks rest on Cordero's knees.

CHAPTER THREE

"So how do you feel?" Melody asked. "Are you glad to be out of the job?"

Reg sighed and took a sip of his coffee.

"Part of me is. I feel like someone has lifted a weight off my shoulders. I should have left a long time ago."

Melody smiled at him. "It's MI6, Reg. You did have the weight of the world on your shoulders, or the country at least."

"I don't know about that, Melody. I don't think any of my operations were of any significance. The place was so secretive, I never knew what else was happening. I signed so many non-disclosure agreements, I don't even remember what I'm supposed to know and not supposed to know."

"And how did Jess take it?"

"Oh, she's okay. She'll carry on working there. She has a good career in front of her. Sometimes I think if I had just stayed where I was, doing what I was doing, I could have made something of it."

"But you didn't, Reg. You've seen more action than most of those tech research guys will ever see between them in a lifetime in the service."

"I didn't want the action, Melody."

"But now you do," she replied. "Now you've had a taste, you wouldn't be happy unless the stakes were high. You were bored out of your mind in there."

Reg turned his cup on the wooden surface of the table, then stared out the window of the coffee shop.

"I just want to do some good, Melody," said Reg. "I know I'm good at what I do. I just want to make a positive impact on the world, and that doesn't mean being shot at or being killed. There's plenty of things I can do. I could go into medical research. I saw a position available online. They're always looking for tech-minded creative individuals apparently, and they're hiring now."

"And what about the other part?"

"Of what?" asked Reg.

"You said a part of you is glad you're out. What about the other part?"

"Oh," said Reg, "yeah, well. The other part is a little more adventurous than the part with the brains."

"You will miss the action then?"

Reg held his finger and thumb in the air and closed the gap until they were an inch apart.

"Maybe this much," he replied with a smile.

"Are you going to take Smokey's offer?"

"Ah, now I see where this is leading," Reg replied. He was sitting back in his chair and let his arms drop to his sides. "You first."

"Me?" said Melody. "Fine. It sounds interesting, and I'm not doing much else right now."

"Don't you think his plan steps over the line of right and wrong?"

"Right and wrong?" said Melody. "No. It

lands somewhere in the grey blur between legal and illegal maybe, but I think he's morally sound. He's got his ear close to the ground, and his finger on the pulse of the black market well enough to assume his intel is legitimate. Besides, he's the chairman of the Society for the Protection of Sacred Arts. He will never do anything to compromise the artwork. All he's doing is saving it for the rest of society to enjoy."

"So you're in then?"

"If you are," Melody replied. "How does that sound? It'd be like old times."

"Don't say that. The last time you said that, I ended up on a gurney seconds away from being embalmed."

Melody laughed, and the woman on a nearby table gave her a disapproving yet questioning look.

The pair laughed again and leaned in close over their coffees.

"So?" Melody asked.

"So what?"

"How about it? Come on. We're a good team. You know we are."

"It does sound like fun," said Reg.

"And his budget is big. You saw the size of the guy's house, right?"

"He said I could have whatever I needed."

"So let's do it," urged Melody. "Come on."

"He already has a tech guy. Fingers."

"Oh, come on. We both know you could wipe the floor with him, and besides, if he's any good, you can have him do all the stuff you don't like doing. Smokey said you'd run the tech operations."

"I have to admit," said Reg, "it's a tempting offer. But what's after this? The time I spend messing around saving these paintings or whatever, I could spend finding a new job."

"Do you think the medical research world will fall to pieces if you don't show up for an interview?"

Reg gave a little laugh.

"You're not that good, Reg," continued Melody. "Besides, this might be the last chance to get your hands dirty and see some real action."

"Oh, behave, Melody," said Reg. "He's asked us to help stop a painting being stolen. How dirty are my hands going to get doing that?"

Reg tipped the remainder of his latte into his mouth and placed the cup back on the table. He swallowed hard and shoved the cup away.

"I bet it'll be over in a few days, and I'll be sitting pretty in an interview in some tech science lab somewhere out in the sticks."

CHAPTER FOUR

"Cordero's a no-show, Dante," said Rosa. She held her mobile phone to her ear with her shoulder while she filed the edge of her nail with an emery board. "He was due in over an hour ago, and his phone is going through to voicemail."

She tossed the board into her handbag, on an old, wooden desk in her tiny office at the back of a mechanic's garage. Outside in the workshop, the loud rattle of the heavy shutters on the back of the truck clanged around the empty space while someone else hammered nails into wooden crates.

"When did you talk to him last?" asked Dante Dumas. His voice was calm as if the news was of no surprise. No doubt, plans were already forming in his mind. Dante's cunning and meticulous plans were his trademark.

"A few hours ago. He was heading into the gallery for a tour." She kicked the door shut to close out the noise from the workshop.

"We planted a guard there," said Dante. His English was better than Rosa's. It was better than the whole team's. Only a twang of Spanish crept through.

"I know. Diego Del Pino. He's a cousin of mine. He's a safe pair of hands."

"So have you spoken to him?" asked Dante.

"His shift finishes at three. He can't take calls at work. He's not even allowed to have his phone on duty. It stays in his locker. But I've messaged him to call me."

"Good. How close are we to finishing the plan?"

"Luckily, Cordero sent through the images of the frame and the placement before he went missing, so we'll be completing it today."

"Camera placement?"

"Cordero didn't get the shots, and Diego can't take his phone on duty."

Rosa heard Dante take a deep breath and let it out slowly. She pictured his nostrils flaring as they did. It was a warning sign.

"So tell me the plan," he said.

"Diego has a kilo of plastic explosives in his locker. Antonio will hack the security system from outside somewhere, disable the cameras and run a dummy loop right about the time that Diego blows the control room door and takes control of the guards."

"What about the guards out on the floor?" asked Dante.

"It's a small gallery. There's only one or two guards on patrol. Antonio will guide the boys and me to where they are and we can take them out."

"'The boys?" said Dante.

"Luca and Marco."

"No. Luca and Marco will not be on the job with you."

"They won't?"

"They're too hot, Rosa. They're straight out of prison and I don't want this job compromised. I'll be with them a few blocks away creating a decoy for you to get away."

"Dante, they're our best guys."

"I said no, Rosa. It's too risky. We'll create a diversion. It's the best we can do."

Rosa paused, carefully choosing her words. She knew Dante's volatility.

"I want you on the job, Rosa. I want you inside. Take Cordero if he surfaces. If not, it'll just be you and Diego."

"Just Cordero?"

"And Diego."

"Dante, can I say something?"

"Do I want to hear it?"

"Dante, this is our last job. This is the big one."

"That's right, Rosa. That's why I want you on it."

"And do we get paid when we're finished? We're all getting a little anxious, Dante. You told us three jobs, and this is the third."

"Rosa, have I ever let you down?"

"No, Dante."

"Do you trust me?"

"Of course, I-"

"Well then, do as I ask. Take Cordero and Diego. What do you need?"

"Get me some tear gas and three gas masks."

"Done," said Dante. "Tell me what happens next, once you've gassed the guards, Antonio has hacked the security, and Diego has control of the guardroom."

"Diego will join Cordero and I. Antonio will cut the sensors and the alarms and then give us the all clear to remove the frame from the wall."

"It will be heavy."

"There's a bolt in the ceiling. We'll use ladders and hang a chain hoist from the bolt to lower the painting to the floor."

"Okay, that's ten minutes."

"Fifteen in total, including taking the guards out," said Rosa.

"Then what?"

"We extract it from the frame."

"Another ten minutes."

"Five," said Rosa. "I'm fast."

"What's the exit plan?" replied Dante, neither agreeing nor disagreeing.

"We'll leave by the front door, get in the van and drive away."

"Door security?"

"Diego has access to the keys, and Antonio will cut the alarms."

"You make it sound easy, Rosa."

"It'd be easier with Luca and Marco."

"You'll be fine. Trust me. With the distraction we have planned, you'll have an open road out of the city."

"One more thing, Dante."

"Go on," he replied.

"I want double."

"You want what?"

"Double," said Rosa. "This whole thing has been planned for the four of us. Now all I have is Cordero, who is still missing, and Diego, who is green behind the ears. It'll be his first job."

"Double is a lot of money."

"The risk is double, the effort is double, the reward is double. It's easy mathematics, Dante."

"I'm leaving you in charge of my lifetime ambition, Rosa. It's the biggest job you'll ever do. Get it right, and I'll see that you never need to work again. Call me when you hear from Cordero. I want to know where he is, and I want you on the road by eight o'clock tonight."

"Of course," said Rosa, but Dante had already disconnected the call.

She tossed her phone onto the desk,

reached across and banged on the thin partition wall.

"Antonio?" she called.

"Sí?" came his response from the small office next door to hers.

"We are go for tonight. Make sure you have that security under control."

"Ah, sí, sí," he replied.

But Rosa's mind was already in Spain, sitting outside her house in the sunshine with her feet up and a glass of sangria in her hand.

CHAPTER FIVE

"I'm a patient man, Cordero," said Harvey. "I can wait all day if I have to."

"Wait then," replied Cordero. "I will tell you nothing."

Harvey smiled.

"So you do know *something*, in which case all I need to do is extract the information from you. I might add that extracting information from people is my specialty."

"I know *nothing*," spat Cordero.

"How are your arms?" asked Harvey. "Tired yet?"

"I'm fine. You think you can break me?"

Harvey let the weight of the two sandbags and gravity pull the sharp point of the hooks into Cordero's skin. Cordero grunted with the additional weight. His legs shook, and he sucked short, sharp breaths through his tight, pursed lips, fighting to control the pain.

"How much do you know now?" asked Harvey. "In time, those hooks will tear through your cartilage, bone and muscle. The longer you hold out, the more painful it will be."

"Fuck you," replied Cordero, in between breaths.

Harvey nodded in admiration at the man's tenaciousness then turned to Smokey.

"Ten minutes, maximum."

"You've done this before?" asked Smokey. His face was calm, but his eyes betrayed his anticipation of what Harvey might do next.

Harvey didn't reply.

Cordero was grunting. He muttered a long string of illegible Spanish.

"What if he doesn't talk?" asked Smokey.

"How bad do you want the information?"

Smokey stared at Cordero hanging from the four lengths of rope and Harvey felt his contempt.

"Do you like art, Harvey?"

"As much as the next guy," Harvey offered, with a slight shrug of his shoulders.

"Well, this man alone is responsible for the loss of millions of dollars' worth of paintings. Some of them will never be seen again, Harvey. But the monetary value isn't the point. It's the art." Smokey seemed to lose himself in his imagination as he spoke. "Think about the time it takes a man to create mind-blowing scenes. Some of them were five hundred years old, four hundred years, three hundred years. And he robbed the world of things that can never ever be returned. Timeless images, Harvey. Timeless."

Harvey didn't reply.

"I want the information, Harvey. Dumas needs to be stopped."

The seriousness is Smokey's eyes spoke volumes.

Harvey lifted two more sandbags with two more butcher hooks.

"Cordero," he said, catching the man's attention, "we know Dumas is planning another robbery. And we know that you know what, where and when. All you have to do is tell us and all of this stops."

Cordero bit his lower lip, fighting the urge to talk, to shout it out.

"It's there, isn't it?" said Harvey. "It's on the tip of your tongue. All you have to do is say the words and I'll let you down."

The statement was met with more rhythmic grunting. Tears had streamed from Cordero's eyes as his shaking body worked the two sharp hooks deeper into his knees.

Harvey collected two more sandbags by the hooks and held them above Cordero's wrists.

Cordero looked up in clear distress, his eyes wide with fear, and the deep carnal grunts, borne from the pit of his stomach, rose in pitch to a fear-fuelled squeal from the back of his throat.

Harvey ran the sharp points along Cordero's skin, creating two faint scratches that drew a thin line of blood on each arm. He stopped with the point of the hooks above Cordero's elbows then watched with intrigue as Cordero fought a battle in his mind. Harvey had seen the battle before. The result all depended on if the battle was with Cordero's own honour and fear, his loyalty to

Dumas, or his fear of what Dumas might do to Cordero should he talk.

The battle played out as if it was on a screen. Cordero's face performed the role of the front line with its desire to deceive Harvey. But his eyes were the stars of the show. He squeezed them closed as Harvey touched the points of the hooks to his skin. If he was holding out for honour, then anger would soon show itself. If he was holding out for loyalty, he would welcome the pain and embrace it. But if he was resisting out of fear of Dumas, his eyes would light up and he would talk.

Harvey lowered the sandbags, letting the weight slip from his hand. The point of the hook sank into Cordero's skin. In just a few seconds, they slipped through his arms to the shank of each hook. Two deep red pools of blood formed on the floor below. But as Cordero screamed and struggled, the hooks in his knees found the sweet spot between the cartilage and the bone. One by one, they too sank deeper into his legs.

The more Cordero struggled and screamed, the deeper the hooks sank, until they could sink no further and hung from his legs, swinging from side to side with his efforts.

Stepping towards the exit, Harvey glimpsed Lola as she ducked out of the garage. He turned to Smokey.

"Maybe we should leave him to think about it for a while," he said.

Smokey's eyebrows raised in admiration of Harvey's control.

Harvey walked towards the door, but he hadn't taken three steps when Cordero broke.

"Okay, okay," he shouted, breathless and hoarse from screaming. "I'll tell you, but let me down."

Harvey returned to his side with two long steps.

"Talk first," he said.

Cordero's face was bright red and shiny with sweat. Four pools of blood had formed on the painted, grey screed floor beneath him.

"No," he begged. "Please, just let me down. I'll talk."

Harvey reached for the last sandbag and picked it up using the last hook.

"I've got one more hook, Cordero," he said, his voice strong and commanding to cut through the man's wailing. "Where should it hang?"

"No, no," Cordero cried. "Please. I'll talk."

"When is the robbery?"

"Let me down, please. I'll tell you any-thing you want, just-"

Harvey offered the hook up to the man's groin.

"How about here?"

"No. No." Cordero's eyes widened further. "It's tonight."

"Where?"

"Just stop. I can't take-"

"Where?" Harvey repeated.

He let the point of the hook rest on Cordero's groin then moved away as Cordero's bladder gave way, and a stream of clear urine soaked his jeans and dripped to the floor. Cordero let the tears roll. At first, a few sorry sobs emerged from his lips, but then the flood gates opened and he cried like a child.

Harvey lifted the hook once more.

"Tell me where, Cordero."

Between a burst of whimpering and a long sniff, Cordero raised his head far enough to look down at Harvey and the point of the hook.

"Last chance," said Harvey.

Cordero spat his phlegm then laughed as Harvey wiped his forearm across his face.

Harvey waited for Smokey's confirmation with raised eyebrows. Smokey returned the silent question with a nod of his head.

Harvey let go of the hook.

CHAPTER SIX

Two gleaming brogues matched Lola's pace. She knew the shoes, knew the walk, and knew the reason he was there. She swam freestyle and increased her speed, yet on each fourth stroke as she raised her head to breathe, the immaculate shoe would be right alongside her.

She coasted the final two metres, grabbed the curved coping stone and leaned on the end of the pool in the shallow end, then tipped her hair back into the water and pulled it over her shoulder. The shoes were standing in front of her. A fresh white towel hung above them and above that was Samuel's face, solemn and expressionless.

"He wants to see me?" Lola asked, as she climbed from the pool and took the towel that Samuel offered.

"Ma'am," replied Samuel.

"I'll be thirty minutes."

"Very good, ma'am," said Samuel. "Will you be accompanying your father for dinner?"

Lola finished towelling herself off, wrapped the towel across her chest, and tucked in the loose end.

"Not today, Samuel. I'll eat alone."

Samuel remained impassive.

"Ma'am, if I might say, your father had asked me-"

"Samuel, I'll eat alone. If we're sending messages via the butler now, you may inform your employer that I shall only talk to him so I can express my disgust, and he should be damn grateful I'm even bothering to do that."

"Indeed, ma'am."

"Thank you, Samuel. That'll be all."

"Very good, ma'am."

Samuel turned on his heels with a practiced flourish, and with arms locked behind his back, he strode alongside the pool to the doors that led into the greenhouse, which connected the indoor pool house and the gym to the west wing of the main house.

Lola pulled a fresh small towel from a pile on a nearby table and dried her hair. She couldn't shake the image of what she had seen earlier that day from her mind. Throwing the towel in the basket, she dropped down onto the edge of a wicker lounger and dropped her face into her hands.

The water had calmed by the time she lifted her head and changed from her bathing suit. She stripped naked by the poolside, strode over to the drying rack and dressed in her favourite soft, baggy, multi-coloured striped pants and a vest top. Then she pulled her damp hair back, shook it to give it some life and stepped into her flip flops before following in the footsteps of Samuel through the greenhouse.

The conservatory, where she knew her father would be, was situated at the end of the east wing. Lola found him, exactly as she'd expected, sitting at the head of the large, twelve-seater dining table. One more place had been set for dinner at the far end of the table. Samuel was standing behind the free chair, ready to seat her.

"Ma'am," he said.

"I told you-"

"Lola, please join me for dinner," her father interjected, without looking up from his dinner. He was sitting with his knife and fork in his hands, but waited courteously for Lola. She shook her head, took her place at the table, and allowed Samuel to push in her chair.

Lola stared down the table at her father while Samuel lifted the cloche from a silver serving dish in the centre of the table. He spooned a healthy amount of roast carrots and broccoli onto a plate, and then selected a few of the leaner, finer cuts of lamb from the dish the cook had prepared.

He placed the plate in front of Lola, poured her water, then stepped back and resumed his position with his hands behind his back.

"Thank you, Samuel," said her father. "That'll be all for the night."

"Ma'am?" said Samuel, offering her a chance for a last request before he retired.

Lola shook her head.

"Very good, sir," said Samuel. He turned on his heels, strode towards the exit into the main house, and pulled the double doors closed behind him.

As soon as the doors clicked shut, Lola fired into action.

"How dare you?" she spat.

"You forget yourself, Lola," her father replied.

"I saw what you did to that man. You had no right."

"I told you to leave."

"I didn't know you hired Harvey Stone," said Lola, almost hushing Harvey's name as if they were being overheard.

"I paid him to do a job, and he'll stay until he's done."

"He's a monster, Dad. I don't want him here."

"He gets the job done," replied her father. "And from what I've seen so far, he's better than most."

"Better?" said Lola. "Better than who?"

"Anyone else I've ever seen."

"So now you're an expert on torture, are you? You're suddenly-"

"You have no idea of the things I've done, Lola. And might I remind you who you're talking to?"

"You've changed. Since you lost your leg, you're different."

"I've always been the same, Lola. But now the stakes are higher."

"It's art, Dad," said Lola quietly, edging on pleading. "For centuries, it's been torn from one hand into the next, stolen, buried, and burned. And it won't stop just because some old Jew in the arse end of England takes it upon himself to call in the big guns and stop one guy from stealing a few paintings. I bet out there right now there's some other thief in some other country nicking some other painting that you've never even clapped eyes on. And what's more, and excuse me for pointing out the elephant in the room, but I've been nicking art in one form or another for years. Bit hypocritical, isn't it?"

Lola's father placed his fork to the side of his plate while he chewed his lamb. Lola waited for him to swallow. He wiped the corners of his mouth with a white napkin.

"If some other thief is, as you say, in some other country, stealing some other art that I am yet to clap eyes on, Lola, there's nothing I can do about that right now. And if I crossed a few lines in my younger years, what can I do now but pay my penance?" He raised his finger, resting his elbow on the table. "But what I can do, right now, right here, in the arse end of England, is stop one man from taking some of the finest artwork this country has to offer. As a result, my girl, millions of others may enjoy the art for perhaps centuries to come."

"If you're so sure it's Dumas, why don't you call the police?"

Her father laughed at the comment and picked up his fork.

"And say what, Lola?" He cut a polite mouthful-sized piece of carrot. "Excuse me, officer, but I happen to know who it was that, just a few weeks ago, stole The Sortie Made by the Garrison of Gibraltar, and The Mother and Child. I don't suppose you could send a squad car round to pick them up, could you?"

"You know what he stole already?"

"Of course I know what he stole, my girl. They were two of my favourite paintings."

"And you're going to send Harvey Stone in to stop him?" asked Lola. "You think he can handle Dumas' men?"

"No, dear. Mr Stone is merely extracting the information. He refused to get involved. I have another team who will handle Dumas when the time is right."

"So you paid him to torture Cordero?"

Her father shrugged.

"We came to an arrangement. I asked him to help with Cordero but he drew the line at Dumas. He said he's tired of it all and wants to go back to his house in France."

"Well, I'm out," said Lola. She wiped her hands on her napkin, and dropped it beside her plate. "I can't work with him. And I can't work with you. Not now."

"You knew he was a violent man. He saved your life, remember?"

"That was different. We were in a situation."

"I need you in this, Lola. Harvey's good, but I need your-"

"My what, Dad?"

"Skills, Lola."

"My skills? Who else have you hired to stop Dumas? I'm guessing they're equally sick?"

"No, they're very different. Together, the four of you make a well-rounded team. Dumas doesn't stand a chance."

"It sounds like Fingers and I are excess. Why would you need four of us?"

Her father shook his head slowly and kept his eyes focused on Lola's.

"Melody Mills and Reg Tenant have skills and links that we do not have. How about it?"

Lola felt her father's manipulation closing in like a ring of guards, each stepping forwards a pace with every word he spoke.

"Of course they have skills. They're ex-police. So you're protecting yourself? But I can't see what help they'd be to stop Dumas."

Her father seemed pleased with the team he was building. The corners of his mouth curled with unconcealed delight.

"They were MI6, my girl."

"They were what? MI6? What the hell do they want with stolen paintings?"

"Nothing. That's the point. Like I said, they have skills and contacts. They'll be helpful."

"You have got to be joking," said Lola. "I knew they were police, but...do you realise what would happen if they recognise most of the paintings in this house?"

"They were MI6, Lola. Unless you can snort it or blow it up, they wouldn't have a clue what it is. In fact, I doubt they'll know a Monet from a Michelangelo."

"I can't do it, Dad. It's got fail written all over it."

"One last time, Lola. It's all I ask."

Lola let the thought of helping her father one last time roll around her head for just a fraction of a moment before reality hit home. She held her hands up in despair.

"Can't you see it? It's crazy, Dad."

"It's what I want. It's what I've always wanted."

"What is?"

For the first time, her father had no reply.

"What's what you always wanted, Dad?"

Silence.

"Dad?"

Her father didn't reply.

"It's it, isn't it? Dumas, he's going to rob the Defeat of the Floating Batteries at Gibraltar, isn't he?"

Her father averted his eyes.

"That's what all this is about," said Lola. "It's not about the art. It's not about you doing good. It's about Dumas stealing the painting that you've always wanted. And you can't have it because now you're the chairman of some art society."

"He needs to be stopped, Lola."

She pushed her chair out, stood up, and began to walk away from the table but stopped, and without turning to face him, she addressed her father for the last time.

"I can't be a part of this."

CHAPTER SEVEN

"Are you okay, Smokey?" asked Melody. "You seem a little off."

Smokey slid himself to one side of his bed in the grand conservatory, lowered his good leg, and then pushed off. He gave a practiced twist, found the arms of the wheelchair and lowered himself into it.

"Smokey?" said Melody.

"I want to show you something," he replied. "Have you finished your tea?"

Melody nodded and looked across at Reg, who sank the rest of his and placed the cup on the small coffee table.

"Let's go into the garden," said Smokey. "I just came inside for a nap and to think. I feel like I've been shut up inside when the weather is this nice. Reg, my boy, would you mind doing the honours and pushing this old chair of mine?"

"Sure," said Reg. "I can think of worse places to be shut up though, Smokey. I've never seen a conservatory so big. It has everything you need."

"Everything except a leg, Reg," replied Smokey. "Let's go out that way." Smokey pointed at the white PVC doors that led onto a wide, flagstone terrace.

Once outside, Melody closed the doors behind them and took in the breath-taking view of Smokey's property. A blue sky with picture-perfect white fluffy clouds framed the expanse of manicured lawns and small clumps of trees. Trimmed hedges and vibrant flower beds lined interweaving pathways that led off in all directions. A small brook cut a shallow gorge through the centre of the land-scape and fed into the lake at the front of the house.

"Let's go," said Smokey.

Melody smiled at his ability to control a situation despite his recent disability. She walked beside him.

"It's a beautiful property, Smokey. Have you owned it for long?" said Melody.

"Too long, I think, Melody. I keep meaning to get rid of it. I have a more modest house in North London. But with a leg gone, I'm not sure I could manage the stairs anymore."

"How could you even consider selling this place?" asked Reg, as he steered the chair onto a small, stone footbridge that spanned the brook. "It's incredible."

"My grandfather bought it, you know? That was before I was born. He had all the money. That damn old miser never let a penny go astray. When my father inherited it, the greed got its hold on him too. We never came here, never visited. The place was left to rot. I took over when my father passed, but it wasn't out of duty or desire, you understand? Oh, no. I took a step through those two front doors for the first time, and my eyes fell onto an oil painting so big and so well-crafted that I was standing on that spot, enthralled by it's magnificence and fell in love. Transfixed, I was. That painting was all I could think about for the longest of times."

"Sounds romantic," Melody said, encouraging Smokey to continue with the story.

"I walked around the house, dumbfounded and bewildered at all the artwork, but I kept going back to the one painting. Like it drew me in."

"So you inherited them? The paintings, I mean. The walls seem to be lined with them."

"I inherited many of them, my dear, and acquired a great deal myself over the years. That's the thing, you see, when you come from nothing and suddenly find yourself surrounded by fine things, you find yourself holding a burning desire. You see something and desire takes over. It grabs you, you understand? And it doesn't let you go until you succumb. Mine is one of the biggest private collections in London now, and as a result, I keep getting voted chairman for the Society for the Protection of Sacred Arts."

"That's quite an achievement, Smokey."

"It's quite a responsibility, Reg. The paintings are considered more valuable than human life sometimes."

"I guess it depends on the human, doesn't it?" Reg joked.

"It often does, Reg," replied Smokey. Then

he muttered to himself, "It often does indeed."

Reg caught Melody's attention, and tapped his temple with one finger, indicating that maybe Smokey had a screw loose.

"I can assure you I have all my faculties, Reg," said Smokey. "I might be crippled, but I'm not stupid or blind."

From the corner of her eye, Melody saw both Reg's shocked expression and Smokey's wry grin, and turned to admire the gardens to hide her amusement.

The path rounded a corner at the end of a long, tall hedge, which had been allowed to grow out. Before them, sitting in a bed of gravel, was a brick-built garage with two huge sliding doors at one end, presumably for vehicles to enter, and a smaller door for foot traffic in the centre.

"I wasn't expecting that," said Reg.

"It's my garage where I keep my classic cars."

"Well, your garage is bigger than all the flats I've ever lived in all rolled into one," said Reg.

Melody held the single door open for Reg to push the wheelchair through, then followed them inside as Reg gave a start and called out.

"Holy mother of-"

"Easy now," said Smokey. "This is what I wanted to show you."

Melody turned from the doors. Her eyes skipped past the classic E-type Jaguar, the sixty-seven Corvette, and the nineteen-thirties Rolls Royce, and landed on a body that hung from thick ropes that reached up into the ceiling void.

Sandbags hung from butcher hooks on the man's limbs. The two that hung from the arms were placed harmlessly over the limbs, but the two hooks at the man's knees had sunk through the cartilage and reappeared at the rear of the leg. One of the man's arms had pulled free of its socket, leaving a grotesque, dislocated deformation that had turned black and blue with a haze of yellow, which had spread across his chest.

A final sandbag hung from a final hook that had been embedded into the man's groin.

A toxic smell of faeces and urine hung like a layer of fog in the air. The man's head hung like the sandbags, an expression of pain and failure etched into his pale face.

"I wasn't expecting that," said Melody.

CHAPTER EIGHT

"Are you guys nearly done here?" Rosa asked. She placed a foot on a stack of two-by-four timbers and leaned on her thigh.

Luca eyed her foot then traced her leg along her knee-length leather boots onto her black skin-tight leggings and up to her chest, which, thankfully, was covered in a loose-fitting checked shirt, tied off in the middle with the sleeves rolled up.

"See anything you like?" she asked him. "How long?"

Luca returned to his work and laughed to himself.

"It's nearly ready," he said, taking a

handful of three-inch screws from a box on the back of the van. He stuffed three into his mouth for safekeeping and screwed the fourth into the two-by-four that he was fixing to the bed of the van.

"Nearly ready doesn't answer my question," said Rosa. "Do you ever give a straight answer?"

"Yeah, well, if I wanted to be asked questions, I'd work in a call centre."

Rosa stood up straight and stepped out of the way as Marco carried another length of timber past her and dropped it next to the one Luca was fixing to the van.

"What's this for?" she asked.

Luca finished screwing in the last screw from his mouth and stood up in the rear of the van.

"It's for the decoy," said Luca.

"I see," said Rosa. "You need a van this big for the decoy?"

"Yes, Rosa, we need a van this big."

Rosa nodded. She was intrigued.

"Are you going to tell me what Dante has planned?"

"No, Rosa. Please excuse us. We are very busy."

Rosa decided to try a different approach.

"It's a shame you guys aren't coming on the last job," said Rosa. "I could do with two safe pairs of hands."

She caught Luca's glance at Marco, and they both lowered their heads without answering.

"Why don't you tell me?" she asked.

Neither replied.

"Is it a secret? I thought we were a team. The first two jobs went well. Why pull you off now? Especially as payday is so close."

"You know this third job is the most important to him?" said Luca.

"Of course. This is the one we've been waiting for. It's the grand prize, which makes it all the more strange that he wouldn't have his two best men on the job."

"The robbery is easy, Rosa. My grandmother could do it."

"But the risk is high," Rosa replied. "The painting is the biggest, the oldest and the most expensive of all of them."

"So you'll need all the help you can get."

"What's that supposed to mean?" asked Rosa.

Luca sighed, stopped working and turned his head to face her.

"We're a decoy, Rosa," Luca whispered. He poked his head from the van and checked around to make sure nobody was nearby. "That's all we know. While you're in the gallery, we'll be somewhere else creating havoc. The attention of the police will be on us, and you will have an easier time of getting away."

"Well why not send the others to do the decoy, and let us three do the job? You know we'll be in and out in less than ten minutes. Who knows how long it will take with the others?"

Luca put his fingers to his lips, gesturing for her to keep the noise down.

"Because, Rosa, Marco and I have been out of prison for exactly three months, and in that time, two very old and expensive paintings have already disappeared like farts in the wind. If we are being watched, which Dante suspects we are, would you like for us to be standing beside you when you take the grand prize? Don't you think that of all the jobs, The Defeat of the Floating Batteries at Gibraltar would be the one that Marco and I would prefer to be on? It would be the highlight of our careers, the encore to our opera of life." He spoke the last words with a flourish, opening his hands and spreading his arms wide.

Rosa considered the statement.

"Alas, we are too hot," Luca continued. "Dante does not want us to compromise the job. But..." He paused, embracing his typical romantic enthusiasm. "We are still helping. We will draw the police in droves, leaving you nothing but empty roads for your escape, and when you are free and clear, you will thank us and we will drink wine."

Luca gave a theatrical bow and the pair laughed at their own humour.

"We are at your service, Rosa," Marco finished.

"You see, Rosa, it is you that will steal our glory," said Luca. "And it will be us that clears the path for you."

"But we will all share the fortune." Marco grinned.

Luca jumped to the ground beside Rosa, dropped to one knee and collected her left hand before Rosa could resist. He kissed it once, holding her gaze with his large brown eyes.

"Is that a straight enough answer for you, my lady?"

CHAPTER NINE

"Who is that?" asked Melody, her voice loud in the huge garage.

"Do you remember I told you about a job I needed help with?" asked Smokey.

"That's the job?"

Smokey laughed.

"No, this is Cordero. He works for a man named Dante Dumas."

"You mean, used to work for Dumas?" said Reg.

From inside the darkened side room, Harvey heard the familiar voices of his old friend, Reg, and Melody, his ex-fiancé. He stood up from his chair, keeping to the shadows, and peered through the small window in the door.

Melody was dressed in her usual black cargo pants, boots, and a tight white t-shirt. She looked good. Unaware of Harvey's voyeurism, Melody began to walk a wide circle around Cordero until she stopped by his feet.

Smokey seemed suitably impressed at Melody's stomach control. Cordero wasn't a pretty sight, but she'd seen worse. She reached out and touched the back of her hand to Cordero's foot.

"He's alive?" she asked.

With a sudden suck of air, Cordero's head raised up, fast and without so much as a warning stir. Melody recoiled. She removed her hand on instinct, then calmed as Cordero held her gaze, pleading with her. Then slowly, he let his head fall to its hanging position.

The sandbags rocked gently back and forth with his movement.

"Cordero has given us information on when and where. All he needs to do is let us know how they plan to steal it, and then we'll let him down."

"It's a painting, right?" asked Reg.

"Not just any painting, Reg," said Smokey. "The Defeat of the Floating Batteries at Gibraltar is considered one of the finest pieces of art of the period."

"What period is it?" asked Reg.

"Ah, you're an aesthete?"

"No," said Reg. "I just wondered how old it is."

Smokey looked up at Melody's gaunt-looking friend, who was standing with his arms hanging by his sides and was dressed in the same old duffel coat he always wore, no matter the weather.

"It was painted by an American called John Singleton Copley in seventeen ninety-one and depicts a failed attempt by the Spanish and French to capture Gibraltar from the British."

"Do you think that's why Dumas wants it? He's Spanish, I presume?" said Reg.

"He would have you think so. He would have you think that it's his heritage, but-"

"But you think otherwise?" said Melody.

"I do," said Smokey. "He is perhaps the most cunning thief of them all. In recent months, since you and I spoke last, Dumas and his crew have stolen two other pieces on two separate occasions. Collectively they are worth a small fortune. But this is his prize. The Defeat of the Floating Batteries at Gibraltar will be the jewel in his collection unless we stop him."

"And that's where we come in?" said Reg.

Smokey nodded.

"That's where I need your help."

"You mentioned his crew. How many are there?" asked Melody.

Smokey rolled himself to a position where he could see both Melody and Reg together. Harvey watched in admiration of Melody as she gathered the facts, exactly as she had always done, and noticed the way she folded her arms, the way she rested her arm on her right hip and rubbed her lips with her left hand when she was thinking.

"Rule number one. Dante Dumas trusts nobody, and nobody trusts Dante Dumas. He has one person who works on nearly every job. The rest are contracted in. He leaves no trail, and he pays well enough that nobody talks."

"He's a pro then?" said Melody.

"He's been in the game long enough that

this won't be a walk in the park. Dumas will be one step ahead the entire time."

"Antonio Rodriguez is his technical genius. He's able to hack into security networks and open up the way for the rest of the team. He's good, and if we can take him down, we may be able to stop Dumas without even leaving the house."

"Sounds like you have an opponent, Reg," said Melody with a smile.

"You're able to hack a security system?" asked Smokey.

Reg's eyes widened as he searched for a modest answer, but Melody interjected.

"He's the best, Smokey," she said. "I've worked with dozens of tech researchers and hackers, and Reg is the best the service could ever offer me."

Smokey nodded with approval.

"That's good to hear. We'll have to see about getting you set up in here."

"What? Near him?" asked Reg, pointing a long bony finger at Cordero.

"Are you squeamish?" asked Smokey in reply.

Melody pushed Reg's hand down and replied on his behalf.

"He'll be fine, Smokey. Tell us about the rest of Dumas' crew."

"Luca and Marco Lopez. Veteran thieves, not just of art. These two could steal the shoes you're walking in. They were released from prison three months ago, coincidently just before the first of the paintings was stolen."

"So they're the men on the ground?" asked Melody.

"Yes. They're strong, smart, and not afraid to use force if need be," replied Smokey.

"Anyone else?"

"Rosa Rivas," said Smokey. "Long-time partner of Luca and Marco. Jewel thief originally, but her path crossed with Dumas during Luca and Marco's trial, and she has been leeching work off him ever since."

"So Rosa Rivas and the brothers are a team?" asked Melody.

Smokey nodded.

"As far as I can make out from our friend over there, they were all brought in to do three jobs. Three paintings. All incredibly expensive. And all high risk."

"They've got two already," said Reg.

"The Defeat of the Floating Batteries at Gibraltar is the jewel in the crown."

"Why is it so difficult?" asked Melody. "I mean, they've got the skills and the head-count. What's all the fuss about?"

"The painting is approximately five metres tall by seven metres wide and is set in a solid bronze frame hanging fifteen feet up on a wall in the Guildhall Gallery in the City of London. It may only be a painting to you, but to some of us, it is the very essence of eighteenth century artwork."

"Where does Cordero fit into this?' asked Melody.

"He's a contractor too. Probably playing the long game, hoping to get something a little more permanent with Dumas."

"Is he going to talk?"

"We're just letting him hang there, giving him time to consider his options."

Melody's head snatched at Smokey's words.

"We?" she said, her face a picture of realisation. "You said we."

"You think I could do this with one leg?" asked Smokey.

There was a long pause as the pieces came together in Melody's mind. She looked at Cordero. The sandbags, the way he'd been tied, even the knots that had been used were familiar.

She spun back to Smokey, her face a blend of terror and joy.

"Where is he?" she asked.

Smokey smiled and raised an eyebrow in innocence.

Harvey pushed open the door.

CHAPTER TEN

"Harvey," said Melody.

She was slightly dizzied at the sight of her ex-fiancé.

"Harvey has been helping me get the information," said Smokey. "He has quite a way about him."

Melody nodded. "I'm familiar with Harvey's ways."

Her statement added to the already electric atmosphere in the garage.

"I'm sensing a history here," said Smokey. His inquisitive gaze switched between Melody and Harvey. "Anything I should know about?"

"No," replied Melody. "We're good."

"Good. Harvey has extracted most of the information. It will be your job to stop Dumas." He turned to Harvey. "Are you sure I cannot tempt you into helping us stop Señor Dumas, Mr Stone?"

Harvey shook his head.

"No. I'm done. The contract was for the information only."

Smokey turned back to Melody and Reg.

"So you see, I need you both."

"Are you going to tell us the plan? I presume that's why we're here today?" said Melody, moving the conversation on.

"Let me explain," said Smokey. He linked his fingers, placed his elbows on the armrests of his wheelchair, and then rested his chin on his fingers. "I've known Dumas for many years, and I also know him to be one of the best art thieves that ever lived. He's cunning, devious, and one of the smartest men you'll ever come across."

"When's the robbery?" asked Reg.

"Tonight."

Reg's confused gaze bounced from Smokey to Melody but avoided Harvey.

"This painting took the artist seven years to complete," Smokey continued. "He was commissioned by the City of London. It is worth a small fortune. Eight figures."

"So our job is to stop him stealing the painting?" asked Melody.

"No. Your job is to catch them stealing it and have them locked up, Miss Mills. Your job, Mr Tenant, is to get Mills into the gallery so she can stop the thieves, and to tie Dumas to the robbery. I need solid evidence. He can't get away."

"With all due respect, Smokey, neither Reg nor I are able to arrest anyone anymore. We quit the service."

"But you know people who can."

"Smokey, are Reg and I here purely because of our links to the police?" asked Melody.

"No, you are both here because of your extraordinary talent at getting into places and because you quite recently were police. Therefore, perhaps we might retain a certain element of ethical practice. I see no reason for us to break the law too much to do what we need to do."

Melody caught a rare grin creeping onto Harvey's face.

"Perhaps we're not the best people for that, Smokey," said Melody. "Our reputation-"

"Your reputation is impeccable."

"You had us checked out?"

"Young lady, you'll find me to be a resourceful man. Although I'm a little limited in my own movements since the leg incident, I still have ways and means. That I do."

"You want me inside the gallery? On my own?" said Melody. "So you do want us to break the law then?"

"Bend it, my girl. Bend it. It shouldn't be too difficult. No, the difficulties will come when you try to stop them. So you'll be armed."

"We're not thieves, Smokey. And we're not police."

"You stole a priceless diamond from the Museum of Natural History, did you or did you not?"

"That was different, Smokey. That was to stop it being stolen."

"So what's different here?" said Smokey. "Instead of a diamond, it's a painting."

"Why don't you just call the law? Make an anonymous call if you're worried it'll come back and bite you," offered Reg.

"The law?" Smokey laughed. "Let's just say that my relationship with the law is fractured, to say the least."

"So why do you need to get in there? Why don't you just wait outside and grab them on the way out?" asked Harvey.

"And risk the painting being damaged? Oh no, my boy, we're going to stop them before it leaves the room."

"What about your daughter and the other guy? Fingers? I thought they'd be in on this," said Reg.

"No, I'm afraid not. The less we say about that, the better. So it's just us. Tell me what you need."

"Plans and security details," said Reg.

"I have them ready up at the house. What about hardware?"

"I have everything I need to hack into the system," said Reg. He patted his satchel.

"Good. So listen carefully. This is how things will go down. Reg here will hack the security, which I might add is extremely sophisticated, so much so that if Dumas' man cannot hack it himself, the whole plan will fail."

"That's a good thing, surely?" said Melody.

"No, my dear, that is a bad thing. It means they won't be able to rob the gallery, which means they won't be locked up, which means they will be free to rob something else. The information I have received is by pure chance. We can't afford to let them get away."

"So you want me to open the doors for them?" asked Reg.

"No, Reg, but loosen them up a bit. Make sure that Dumas' man thinks he's done a good job. Make it easy. Do you know what I mean?"

Reg nodded, slowly falling in with the plan.

"Once they're in, Melody will follow. The painting is big, very big. All we need is for them to lower it to the ground and we have them."

"If they resist?" asked Melody.

"Then do what you need to do," said Smokey, without hesitation. "Disable them, tie them up, leave them for the police, and get out of there. Once you're out, Reg will trigger the alarms and the slam doors will come down, trapping them inside."

"We'll need transport," said Reg. "I'll need to be close by."

"We have a van. What else do you need?"
Smokey turned to Melody.

"Details of Dumas' men. How many and
who," she replied.

Smokey nodded and turned to Harvey.

"Harvey, my boy, it's time to get to work."

CHAPTER ELEVEN

"It's hard not to be impressed, isn't it?" said Lola, as she stared up at the huge painting. "You know, when the gallery was rebuilt, they actually designed the place around this painting, knowing that it would need a wall this big to hang on."

"It is impressive, Lola," replied Fingers, "which is more than I can say for the security."

"Yeah, I thought the same," said Lola. She then whispered, "Does it make you wonder what's downstairs in the control room?"

"How do you know it's downstairs?" asked Fingers.

Lola grinned.

"Professional interest," she said.

"What did you do, Lola?"

"Nothing major. I just took a look at the plans and a security report."

"Where did you get them from?" asked Fingers, apparently hurt that she didn't go through him to obtain the information.

"Dad had them. He is the chairman of the society, you know. I tell you what though, on the outside this place looks like a walk in the park, but behind those walls is so much security you couldn't pass wind in here without half of London's police jumping on you."

"Tell me more," said Fingers. He leaned on the handrail of the mezzanine floor and looked down to make sure nobody was around.

"Okay," said Lola, and leaned forwards to join him. "The control room is at basement level. Eight guards man the desks at all times, twenty-four seven, three hundred and sixty-five days a year. They're monitoring seventy-two high-definition security cameras that cover every square inch of the gallery three times and across three different networks. So if at any time one CCTV system is down, two more are there to cover the space."

"Smart," said Fingers. "And expensive."

"The control room also monitors an array of sensors fixed to the back of every single painting."

"How many paintings?" asked Fingers.

"Over four thousand."

"Four thousand sensors?"

"Not including the pressure sensors in the floor."

"All manned by those eight guards?"

"Yep."

"So surely the way in would be to take over the control room?" said Fingers. "If the tech guy knew his stuff, you'd have free rein over the place."

"Easier said than done," said Lola. "The guards sit inside a self-contained unit. Fireproof, bullet proof, bomb proof, you name it. There's no way in until shift change, when they are escorted by private security, a bunch of ex-special forces guys probably. The doors are locked and sealed until twelve hours later."

"What about the guards on the floor?"

"Basic security. They are literally just a walking pulse ready to hit the alarms."

"And when they do?"

"The slam doors and windows are activated, closing all exits. A direct link to the police obviously sets them in motion while the thieves sit in here and contemplate their bleak futures."

"Well, looking at the lovely paintings at least," said Fingers.

"There's more," said Lola. "If explosives are used, the security system even shuts down the underground and the ring of steel around the City."

"The what?"

"The ring of steel. The barriers all raise. No cars in or out on the roads and the trains come to a grinding halt. The entire square mile of the City is protected by it. The policy started off with the Bank of England but it was extended to other buildings. The City essentially goes into lockdown as soon as an explosion occurs. If you had a painting, this is where you'd want to keep it."

"How many men does this Dumas have?" asked Fingers. "And why is your dad even bothering to try to stop him? The chances of success are minute."

"I don't actually know how big his team is, but the way my dad talks about him, if anyone is capable of pulling this off, it's Dumas. His team is good. They're pros. He would have been planning this for months."

The pair returned their gazes to the painting.

"It's not even my favourite," said Fingers. "It's impressive yes, but-"

"I know what you mean," said Lola. "It's my dad's favourite. And it's Dumas' favourite. Dad has always wanted it, but even he doesn't have that kind of money, and it'll likely never be up for sale anyway."

"Makes you wonder what Dumas wants with it, doesn't it?" said Fingers.

Lola gave a soft, half-hearted laugh. Then she thought back to the last conversation she'd had with her father.

"Dumas wants it for two reasons. The first, because he can, and only he can."

"And the second?"

"Because my dad wants it."

"They know each other?"

"They've been enemies for years, Fingers," replied Lola. "This is the culmination of about three decades of hate, contest, and spite."

"But what's Dumas going to do with it? I mean, it's a bit big to have on the average bedroom wall."

"He'll sell it, and it'll stay on the black market, at least for the rest of my dad's lifetime."

"Why are they enemies? Three decades, man. Get over it and move on, right?"

"You'd think. The way I understand it is that Dumas and my father both worked for some guy when they were younger. They were both thieves, you know?"

"Your dad was an art thief?"

"One of the best, Fingers, as was my grandfather, at least until he could afford to buy his own art. My father is not proud of what he did, but you can't change the past. I think that's why he took the chairman job, to put something back into the art community."

"Yeah, but did he give the stolen paintings back?" Fingers smirked.

"Every one of them. In fact, you're looking at one of them," said Lola. "Now he's dead set on protecting the world's artwork. It's almost like a mission in life."

"Your father stole this?"

"My grandfather stole it. My father returned it. Now Dumas wants to steal it and my father has dug his heels in."

"I don't think we need to worry too much

about this being stolen again," said Fingers, nodding at the huge painting before them. "I'll see if I can get into the security and take a look around. I could probably set up a sniffer to alert us when Dumas' men hack in."

"You can do that if you want," said Lola. "But I told my dad last night, I'm out. I don't want anything to do with it."

"What? Why not?" said Fingers. "You just told me it's your dad's favourite painting. I thought we were going to help him stop Dumas?"

Lola contemplated her next words carefully.

"He's my father, Fingers, and I love him. But sometimes..." She paused and looked away to brush a tear from her eye.

"Sometimes?" said Fingers.

"He's gone too far, Fingers. He needs to be shown that money can't buy you everything. Maybe if he loses something close to his heart, he'll re-evaluate his priorities."

The pair took the wide staircase down to the ground floor, turning away from the huge painting and walking out through the main doors onto Basinghall Street. They turned left and crossed the road, where a man stopped them for directions. He spoke in Spanish and seemed agitated.

"No hablo español," said Lola.

But the man's face just broadened into a smile. His eyes darted behind Lola just as a loud screech of tyres filled the street. Lola spun to find an unmarked white van on the road two feet behind her. The side door slid open to reveal two wooden crates. Just as Lola turned to run, she felt a dull thump on the back of her head.

Somewhere, as darkness began to envelop her sight, she saw Fingers fall to the ground beside her. Her own knees buckled. Two hands grabbed beneath her arms as she fell. Unconsciousness took her before she could offer any further resistance.

CHAPTER TWELVE

"Go easy on him, Harvey," said Smokey. "He's no use to us dead."

Harvey didn't reply. Instead, he wandered outside through the single door to a small wood pile. The pile had clearly been made by the gardener or groundsman. It consisted of felled fern trees cut into foot-long logs and a larger pile of dried branches, brown and ready to burn.

He collected an armful of logs and two large, bushy branches then stepped back inside the building.

Cordero hung motionless. His bruised limbs had begun to turn a very unhealthy yellow. His head hung back as if he was peering backwards, but in reality, he no longer had the strength to raise it.

Harvey dropped the woodpile on the floor.

"Harvey, what are you doing?" asked Melody.

Harvey didn't reply.

"He's getting answers, my dear," said Smokey. "It's quite fascinating to watch."

"I've seen Harvey get answers before," replied Melody. Then she turned back to Harvey. "You don't need to do this."

Harvey didn't reply.

Instead, he began to lay the logs side by side in a line beneath Cordero.

"Harvey, no. I can't allow this," said Melody, her voice growing in urgency.

"You can leave if you wish," said Smokey.

Harvey snapped the branches into smaller pieces to form a tinder and lay them over the logs. Eventually, the scene was set.

"Please don't do this, Harvey," said Melody.

Harvey raised his head for the first time. His eyes met Melody's and he winked.

Melody remained silent.

Harvey reached for the single length of

rope that ran through the system of pulleys and untied the figure of eight that held Cordero suspended. He lowered Cordero closer to the wood.

The movement seemed to rouse the Spaniard. His groggy eyes fell on Harvey but saw through him as if he was unable to focus.

Soon, the sandbags that hung from his limbs touched the ground, removing the weight from his knees and elbows. But Cordero's elation was short lived as the sharp end of the chopped wood pricked his skin.

"When?" said Harvey.

Cordero exhaled, long and deep. Relief washed over his agonised face.

"I can make the pain go away," said Harvey. "I can make all this stop."

Cordero ran his feeble tongue across his parched and cracked lips.

"Melody, I need some water," said Harvey, without removing his eyes from Cordero. In the corner of his eye, he saw Smokey gesture to the rear wall where a six-pack of large water bottles were standing beside a kettle on an immaculate black work surface.

"Here," she said, offering him the bottle with an outstretched arm.

Harvey took the bottle, removed the cap and poured water from a standing height onto Cordero's face, being careful not to get the wood wet. Cordero came alive. He kicked out, wrenched his arms against their restraints, turned his head from side to side and coughed up a mix of clear bile and water that ran across his face and hung in a long gloopy string.

"When?" Harvey repeated.

Panting for breath, Cordero raised his head to stare at Harvey who loomed over him, expressionless.

"Fuck you," Cordero croaked. "Untie me and I'll talk."

Harvey tipped the bottle up once more, letting the water run across Cordero's mouth and nose until he gasped for air. His body convulsed and once more, clear bile ran from his mouth.

The bottle was empty. Harvey tossed it to one side. It clattered across the hard concrete floor and settled in the corner of the garage.

"So we'll do it the hard way," said Harvey. His voice betrayed neither disappointment nor pleasure.

He pulled once more on the rope, raising

Cordero back into the air. The sandbags swung, tearing at his skin, and Melody turned away as Cordero's contorted face let out an agonised scream of renewed pain.

Harvey tied the rope off once Cordero was above his head. Bile, water and urine dripped from Cordero's broken body. Producing a box of matches from his pocket, Harvey removed one and slid the cardboard packet shut.

"How many men?" asked Harvey.

The only sounds that came from Cordero were whimpers, grunts, and some kind of screeching that formed in the man's gut. The grunts grew loud, forming a rhythm. As they pulsed, Harvey imagined the pain that shot through Cordero's body with every loathsome beat of his weakened heart.

Harvey struck the match, letting the smell of burned sulphur drift into Cordero's face.

More urine leaked from Cordero's pants.

"How many?" Harvey repeated once more.

"Let me down," came the reply, feeble but full of anger.

The match burned out. Dead wood smoke carried to Cordero's nose and his nostrils flared with the realisation of what was about to happen.

Harvey retrieved another match from the box. But as he struck the match, Smokey's hand raised to silence the room. Harvey let the match burn and averted his gaze to the man in the wheelchair who was sitting listening to a call.

Smokey's face dropped. The lines etched into his forehead and surrounding his tired eyes all fell with gravity. His mouth sagged open, his eyes closed shut, and he dropped the phone onto his lap.

Harvey remained by Cordero's side.

"Smokey?" said Reg. "Who was that?"

"Are you okay?" asked Melody. "You look like you've seen a ghost."

With a visible effort to control the emotion in his voice, Smokey removed his glasses, pinched the bridge of his nose, then wiped his eye and looked up at Harvey, as if he was the only person in the room.

He took a swallow, then spoke softly, but loud enough for Harvey to hear.

"They've got Lola."

CHAPTER THIRTEEN

The garage suddenly filled with Cordero's cackle, a laugh that seemed to jab sharp spikes of hate into Smokey's sullen demeanour.

Melody tore herself away from Cordero and pulled a blank-faced Reg from where he'd been standing, not daring to move for the past fifteen minutes as he had watched Harvey work.

"Reg, let's go. Now," she said.

Reg was shaken from his daze.

"Laptop. Find her."

He immediately fell in with Melody's idea. Within a few moments, Reg's laptop was out of his satchel and opened up on the wing of a bright red, nineteen sixty-two, E-type Jaguar. He pulled a mobile Wi-Fi hot-spot from his bag, clicked the switch on and watched the row of lights flash as they sought an internet connection. After a few seconds, they stayed solid to indicate a signal had been found; three of the five lights stayed on.

"Sixty percent signal. Should be fine," said Reg.

"Find her mobile phone," said Melody to Reg, then she turned to Smokey. "Smokey, listen, we're going to need to know everything that happened, where she might have gone, and who she might have been with."

Smokey stared at the floor then raised his head, seeming to peer through Melody.

"Smokey," said Melody again, "you need to be strong now. We can find her but we need your help."

She had to raise her voice to be heard over Cordero's impassioned and uncontrollable laughter. The Spaniard rocked from side to side in his crazed state as he hung from his bindings, causing the sandbags to find a motion of their own. For a split second, Melody held Harvey's gaze, but then he turned to Smokey, who simply nodded his request.

"Smokey, help us find her," Melody shouted.

Harvey lit a match.

Cordero, seemingly oblivious or hardened to the pain of the hooks through his knees, gave a maniacal screech that filled the room.

"Smokey?"

Harvey dropped the match to the hungry dry ferns.

"Now you'll see," cried Cordero, between fits of raving lunacy. "Now you'll see who's smarter, you old cripple."

"I have her signal," called Reg from the cars behind Melody. "She's moving fast."

"Where?" Melody replied, leaving Smokey to his dreamlike state.

Smoke started to rise up, engulfing Cordero in thick, grey plumes as the ferns began to take flame.

"London. She's in the City," said Reg.

Suddenly, without warning, Cordero's maniacal laughter rose an octave. The crackle of burning wood filled the spaces between as he inhaled a lungful of smoke, coughed, and wheezed for air. His body contorted in wild thrusts as the heat began to sear his skin.

"All of them," yelled Cordero. "It's tonight. They'll all be there. Five of them."

"And Dumas?" said Harvey.

But Cordero burst into frantic, frustrated fits as he tried to escape the heat that was growing beneath him.

"Yes. Yes. He'll be there. Now get me down, please," cried Cordero.

"What time?" asked Harvey. "Tell me and I'll put a stop to it all."

"Fingers," said Smokey, suddenly and without warning.

Melody and Reg's heads spun to find the old Jew, fully composed and staring back at them.

"She's with Fingers," he repeated.

With a few deft swipes of his laptop's track-pad and several clicks of the mouse, Reg had Fingers' contact file open. He copied the mobile number into his tracking software and hit enter.

"Eleven o'clock," screamed Cordero. "It's eleven tonight."

"Why take Lola?" asked Harvey, his voice the calmest in the room.

"Let me down, please," begged Cordero. "I told you what you need to know."

A particularly bushy branch of fern began to catch light. The flames spread across its length, devouring the dead bristles and growing higher.

"Why take Lola?" Harvey asked again.

"Dumas has taken Lola because he knows I'll concentrate my efforts on finding her," said Smokey. He rolled towards where Cordero hung then gestured to Harvey at a wide broom that leaned against the wall.

"They'll kill her," said Cordero, "if you don't let me go."

"That's enough, Harvey," Smokey said.

Harvey didn't reply.

"Harvey, I said that's enough. Move the fire."

Melody and Reg both looked up from the laptop at the tension that was now evident.

The thick, acrid smell of burning flesh had begun to overwhelm the rich aromatic taste of burning evergreen. Cordero had ceased to scream or squeal and had resorted to exhausted whimpers.

Melody made herself ready as Harvey and Smokey were locked in a stare.

"Harvey, please move the fire," said Smokey.

Harvey waited a moment, then nodded, and fetched two bottles of water to extinguish the flames. Cordero hung lifeless in the midst of thick smoke.

With a questioning look on his face, Harvey stared over Cordero's broken form at Melody.

"What is it, Harvey?"

Smokey and Reg turned to face Harvey, who stared back at Melody.

"Harvey, talk to me," said Melody. She knew that look. She knew what his gaze meant.

"I'm in," he said.

Melody nodded in reply.

As if satisfied with the response, Harvey's gaze fell on Smokey.

A silence ensued. All eyes fell on Smokey. All Harvey needed was the go-ahead to make his move. Melody would be by his side. Reg could guide them in.

"What do you think, Smokey?" said Melody. "I can't get her back alone."

After some deliberation, and with steepled fingers held beneath his chin, Smokey finally turned to Reg and spoke.

"Are you able to get into the gallery's security system?"

Slightly taken back to have a question directed at him, Reg stammered but replied with caution.

"Sure," he said.

"Melody and Harvey will need passes."

"Passes?" said Melody. "Smokey, Dumas has Lola-"

"And if we don't stop him, he'll have the painting too."

"What's more important to you, the damn painting or your daughter?" said Melody, disgusted at his nonchalance.

"Lola is my whole world, my dear," said Smokey. "But if we go after her, we'll be playing right into Dumas' hands. No. No, we stop him. We stop the robbery. It's the last thing he'll be expecting."

"And Lola?" asked Melody.

"Lola's a tough girl. Something tells me there's more to this than we know."

"You're risking your daughter's life for a painting, Smokey. If she survives, she'll never forgive you. If she doesn't, you'll never forgive yourself."

"My dear, if we go chasing after her,

Dumas will have us running around London, at least until they have the painting. Then we'll be nowhere but a laughingstock. No, that's not how it happens. We stop the robbery." He turned from Melody, bringing the conversation to a halt. "Reg, can you do it?"

"I'm into the back end of the security system now," replied Reg. "I'm adding Melody and Harvey to the security records. Plus I managed to hack into the supervisor's email account to notify the control room, letting them know that there will be two new guards tonight. It looks like the floor is guarded by a different firm to the control room. It's a split security strategy that minimises the risk of internal corruption. But it also means that the guards in the control room are used to seeing strangers from the other firm covering the gallery duty."

"What time does the shift start?" asked Melody.

"Ten," said Reg.

"It's seven thirty now," said Melody. She turned to Harvey who was leaning against the wall. "We've got two and a half hours to get there, find uniforms and get onto the floor."

Harvey didn't reply. He nodded, shoved

off the wall, and gave Smokey a look as if offering him a silent chance to voice any last changes.

Smokey returned the stare, then offered a single indiscernible nod.

Harvey began to move towards the door.

"Reg, keep an eye on Lola and Fingers," said Melody as she hurried after Harvey.

"Wait," said Smokey.

The pair stopped.

Smokey wheeled himself to a bright red tool chest that was standing by a bench in front of his impressive line of cars. He opened the bottom drawer and pulled out two black cases that Melody recognised immediately.

"You might need these," he said.

Both Harvey and Melody took a larger case each. Inside each was a single SIG Sauer P226 with two magazines. Smokey pulled two small boxes of ammunition from another drawer and handed them across to Harvey and Melody. Harvey loaded his weapon and stuffed the spare magazine into the pocket of his cargo pants.

Reg then passed them a smaller case, from which, Melody produced two GPS earpieces.

"Wear these. I can track you from here," said Reg.

"Are we ready?" asked Harvey.

"Reg, are we good to go?" Melody asked.

"I'm set," he replied, pulling his headphones from his bag. "But what do we do about Cordero? He's still alive." He gestured at the broken Spaniard who still hung from the ropes. His skin was charred and bruised and his breathing was shallow, but it was deep enough that they could see the faint rise and fall of his stomach.

Melody glanced at Smokey, who in turn looked at Harvey.

Reading the signal exactly as it was intended, Harvey approached Cordero, raised his weapon and fired two shots, one in his chest, and one in his head.

He turned back to Melody.

"Are we ready now?" he said.

CHAPTER FOURTEEN

It wasn't the first time Lola had been trapped in the back of a van.

She came to as the van took a right-hand bend, which rolled her onto her side and sent a hot wave of nausea through her gut. Stomach acid clawed at her throat and trickled into her mouth. She spat into the darkness, blind as to the direction.

"You're awake," said a man's voice. "That was fast." His dialect had a lick of romance, which Lola guessed to be Spanish, well disguised but recognisable.

"You're wondering where you are," he said.

Lola felt the wooden floor beneath her.

She sat back and leaned against two large wooden crates.

"I'm in a van," she replied. "Open the door and I'll tell you where exactly."

"You have your father's humour, Lola. It's a good trait to have, but it is useless with nothing to support its enthusiasm."

Lola judged him to be sitting on the wheel arch a few feet away. She felt for the bump on her head, then winced when her fumbling fingers found it.

"What is it you want, Dante?" She held her head steady in her hands, trying to control the dizzying sensation.

"Your mind, Lola."

"Is this about Cordero?"

"Cordero? Oh, so your father does have him? And I'm guessing he now thinks he has control? But you will see who is in control, Lola."

"I'd be surprised if Cordero is even still alive," said Lola. "Last I saw of him, he was having a pretty awful time of it."

"And the last I saw of him, he was planning to betray me," Dante countered.

"You think he'd betray you?"

"I know he'd betray me. In fact, I'm counting on him betraying me."

Lola tried to piece together what Dante was saying, but her head pounded, and she fought to hold back the nausea.

"Don't try to understand it, Lola," said Dante. "It'll all become apparent in a short while."

"My father will stop you. He'll throw everything he has at bringing you down, and he'd die rather than see the painting in your hands."

"The painting?" said Dante. "Oh, you mean The Defeat of the Floating Batteries at Gibraltar? Yes, he would. You see, we've both always had a kind of affinity for the piece. It is, after all, a masterpiece."

"You won't get it, Dante," said Lola. "Why don't you stop now? You know he'll kill Cordero if it means stopping you."

The van slowed, the driver cut the engine, and the vehicle shuddered to a stop.

"You're right, Lola. I won't get it. And if he kills Cordero, well, he'll be saving me a job."

The side door of the van slid open, but Lola wasn't blinded by a dazzling light; they were parked in a side street with tall buildings that cast the cobbled road in shadow.

Two men were standing in front of the door, blocking Lola's escape. The man on the right tossed her a pair of coveralls.

"Put these on," he said. His Spanish accent was thicker than Dante's. The tail end of the sentence was drawn out, and his esses were more pronounced.

Lola stood up, half crouched, and tried to duck out of the van.

"Are you going to move out of the way?" she asked.

"Marco, let her out. She won't run," said Dante, as he too made to exit the van. For the first time, Lola noticed that Dante was also wearing coveralls. In fact, they all were.

She buttoned up the over-sized coveralls, rolled the sleeves back and put her hands on her hips.

"So I've got the uniform. Now what?"

The other man threw her a hard hat, the likes of which she'd seen construction workers wear. Then the men set to unloading large canvas bags from the van, which clanged when they hit the ground with the unmistakable sound of heavy tools.

"Now, we wait," said Dante, checking his watch. "Antonio, are you joining us?"

A fourth man, slighter than the others, slid from the front seat of the van. He clutched a laptop bag and pushed his glasses onto the bridge of his nose with a habitual touch.

"What are we waiting for?" asked Lola.

"Dante, do we really need her?" said the man who'd thrown her the hat. "She asks too many questions."

"We need her, Luca," replied Dante. "Just wait and you will see."

Dante checked his watch again. Lola instinctively checked hers. It was ten forty-five.

"Okay, it is time," said Dante. "Luca, Marco, get the bags. Antonio, be ready for Rosa's call. And Lola, please do not try to run. I can assure you that Marco and Luca here will catch you."

Lola's heart began to pump. It was the same feeling she got before a job. Adrenaline began to line the walls of her veins and her hands became clammy. Dumas held out his hand.

"Your phone," he said. "I imagine your friends will be looking for you."

Seeing no gain from arguing, Lola pulled her phone from her pocket and handed it over. But instead of throwing it into the van, Dumas placed it on the wooden crate that had been pushed against the bulkhead.

"That'll lead them to a dead end," he said with a smile.

The van doors were slammed shut. Dante led the way with Luca and Marco taking up the behind. Antonio walked beside Lola but said nothing. As soon as they left the small side street, evening sunlight warmed her face. Lola recognised the area as Cannon Street.

"Are you tunnelling into the gallery?" she asked. "It's a long way."

No reply followed. None of the men reacted at all.

A short walk later, the five entered Cannon Street Station. Antonio handed Lola an Oyster card to swipe through the barriers, and soon, they were descending the escalators along with city workers who'd either had a few drinks after work or worked late. Most people seemed to be alone. But there were a few groups who were louder than necessary, their smart office ties pulled loose.

At the foot of the escalators, the London

Underground platforms were left and right, and signs for the overhead main lines pointed back up to ground level.

"This way," said Dante, and the group followed without stopping. Dante's stride was confident as he approached a single door in the wall. He unlocked it, pulled it open and stepped aside to allow his team and Lola to enter before closing it behind him and locking it again.

The door opened into a well-lit, tiled corridor that bore the signs of many years of use by the engineers that maintained the station and the railway lines. Lola guessed it was some kind of service tunnel to the various service areas of the station. It would lead to the power station, the switch room and the escalators, and likely to the actual underground tunnels themselves.

"Antonio, it's time for phase one," said Dante.

The smaller man pulled his laptop from his bag, then opened a panel that was housed in the wall. Inside were various switches and connection ports. He connected a network cable from the laptop to the interface on the panel, waited a few seconds, and then announced that he was online. He then connected his phone to the laptop and set it down to one side.

"We're ready," he said.

"Good," said Dante. "Now it is time for a little mayhem."

CHAPTER FIFTEEN

London's night time lights shone bright and true. Black cabs dominated the roads, city workers dominated the walkways, and in the back streets of the city, only the occasional stumbling drunk or homeless wanderer were to be seen.

It had been an hour since Luca had stopped the van for Rosa to get out, and then he, Dante, Marco and Antonio had driven on to the decoy.

Rosa dialled a number from memory on the burner she'd been given, placed the hands-free earpiece in her ear, and waited for Antonio to answer.

"Three minutes, Antonio. Is Diego in position?"

"Sí, Rosa. He is ready and waiting."

"Okay, at precisely eleven, he is to blow the door to the control room, and you are to disable the alarms on the basement entrance for me."

"Sí, Rosa. Everything is ready."

A couple, neither drunk nor homeless, turned into the street and walked towards her. The man's silhouette showed a confident, unhurried walk. The woman linked her arm with his and leaned into him.

Rosa stepped back into the doorway of an office block opposite the gallery.

She watched as the couple crossed the small street and passed her without looking up. Rosa waited for them to pass and for their voices to fade.

"Okay, we're ready. I'm going to the basement level now."

The gallery's arched doorway was standing in front of her. Thirty feet to her right was a small iron staircase that led to the basement dent. Rosa checked left and right, darted across the road then took the iron stairs down to a dark entrance.

"Rosa."

"Yes, Antonio," she whispered.

"You are at the door?"

"Yes."

A loud buzzer came from inside, and a small click indicated that the electromagnet had been released. Rosa pushed the door, stepped inside and closed it behind her. A cloud of thick, acrid smoke and the smell of explosives hung in the air. Beyond a glass wall to her right was her cousin Diego. He was standing at the controls with a crazed look on his face. The adrenaline pumping through him made his eyes large and black. Eight guards lay slumped over their desks around him.

He signed that everything was running to plan. Rosa nodded in reply.

"Control room is down. Antonio, kill the alarms and sensors. We're going into the gallery now." She turned back to the control room. "Diego, stay with me," she called, then waited for Diego to emerge from the smoke-filled glass room.

"Antonio, I need eyes on the gallery. Where are the guards?"

"Okay, Rosa. There is one guard at the top

of the central staircase. The other is on the ground floor by the main entrance. If you climb the staircase beside the control room, you will enter the gallery on the ground floor beside the second guard. I would suggest one of you takes the staircase to the first floor so you can each take one guard."

"Good call, Antonio," said Rosa. She dropped her heavy backpack, pulled out two gas masks and two canisters of tear gas, and then handed one of each to Diego.

"First floor. There's a guard on the left as you enter the gallery. Put this over your face, pull this pin from here, and toss the canister towards him."

Diego was fired up, breathing heavily, and snatched the items from Rosa's hands.

"Hey," she said, stopping him from running up the stairs. "Are you wearing a watch?"

"Sí," he replied.

"Okay, thirty seconds from..." She held out for the minute hand on her watch to hit twelve. "Now."

Diego took the stairs two at a time and disappeared from sight. Rosa walked calmly behind him. She stopped at the ground floor and checked her watch again.

Ten seconds.

She readied herself and pulled the mask over her face.

Five seconds.

She put her hand on the handle and peered through the glass.

One.

CHAPTER SIXTEEN

All it took was a nod of Harvey's head to the guards behind the glass screen, and a smile from Melody, for the process to begin like a routine. A clipboard was passed through a stainless steel security drawer. The pair filled in the spaces and passed it back with their fresh identification cards, which Reg had printed just two hours previously.

"You pulled graveyard duty, did you?" asked the guard at the screen.

"Looks that way, doesn't it?" said Harvey, with an accompanying glare. One of the other guards looked up from his desk. He pulled the ID cards from the drawer and began to run their details through the security system.

"Well, it could be worse, mate," said the first guard, as the second began typing their names.

"Is that right?" said Harvey. "And how exactly could it be worse?"

He felt a soft kick from Melody beneath the counter. The guard's humour stopped. He began to study Harvey and Melody's faces, then glanced at his colleague who had found the dummy profiles that Reg had planted on the security interface. A mugshot of both Harvey and Melody filled one screen with a line of text below each photo, too far away to read.

"Don't mind him," said Melody. "He's just grouchy because he won't get his pie and mash tonight. I'm Melody, by the way."

"Pie and mash?" asked the guard, his face twisted with misunderstanding.

"Yeah, we usually work at the Science Museum. They have a cafeteria we can use during our breaks. Harvey here is fond of the pie and mash."

"And you've been pulled off your pie and mash gig to come and spend the night here?"

Harvey didn't reply.

"Well," continued the guard, "you can use the vending machine by the main entrance if you want a pissy cup of lukewarm coffee. There's two more guards from your firm up there already. I'll let them do a handover. They'll show you where everything is."

The second guard tossed the passes back into the security drawer, and the first guard dropped in two walkie-talkies along with two thick plastic key cards. He slammed the drawer shut, allowing Harvey and Melody access to the passes and allocated equipment from their side of the glass screen.

"But it doesn't do pie and mash, I'm afraid," he finished, with a half-smile aimed at Harvey who held his smug gaze.

"Thanks. What do I call you?" asked Melody.

The guard switched his attention to Melody.

"You don't," he replied. "Shift changes in eight hours. One of you upstairs, one of you downstairs. No chatting. We'll be watching." He gestured over his left shoulder at the row of guards behind him, all with their backs to the front desk. Each of them had two screens that showed a variety of camera views and digital readouts from the sensors placed around the gallery.

"Looks high tech," said Melody.

"You fart and we'll know," replied the guard with a wink.

Melody clipped her walkie-talkie onto her belt.

"I'll bear that in mind" she replied with a roll of her eyes. "Come on, Harv."

"Through those doors and up the stairs. We do a comms check every hour on the hour. Don't miss it, eh?" said the guard, as the door to the stairwell closed behind Harvey.

They took the stairs slowly, aware of the flashing LEDs of the cameras fixed to the corners of the ceiling. Making a show of scratching his ear, but hitting the tiny button on his earpiece, Harvey opened the communications channel between Melody and himself.

"You take the ground floor. I'll take the top," said Harvey.

"Copy that," said Melody, who already had her channel open.

Harvey climbed the stairs to the first floor and listened for the beep and click of the ground floor door's magnetic lock as Melody entered downstairs. Then he swiped the card he'd been given and stepped through into the gallery.

The space was open-plan and rectangular. To his right was a long wall lined with paintings, dimly lit, but enough to see by, with soft, patterned carpet underfoot. To his left, thirty feet away, was a sweeping staircase leading down to the ground floor. A guard was standing at the opposite end of the room, leaning over the balcony and looking down. A faint murmuring of voices could be heard.

The door closed behind him with a click.

"Hola," said the guard, turning his head to face Harvey, but retaining his casual position. He looked tall, not particularly well-built, but confident. The Spanish greeting caught Harvey's attention.

"Is this it?" asked Harvey.

"Sí, this is it, my friend," the guard replied. "Nothing but a big empty room to keep you company."

The guard turned back to look over the edge.

"So I'm here now," said Harvey. "Which means you can go."

"Sí," replied the Spaniard, but he didn't move.

Taking a step forwards, Harvey glanced over the edge as the guard Melody had replaced pushed the stairwell door open, leaving her to work the next shift.

Seeing his colleague leave, the first-floor guard pushed off the balcony, rolled his neck and breathed in. In the air-conditioned room, his warm and stale coffee breath reached Harvey from a few feet away.

"You're supposed to give me a handover or something," said Harvey.

"A handover?" replied the guard. He looked Harvey up and down as if sizing him up. "What do you need to know? The washroom is downstairs, the coffee is terrible, and there are no chairs to sit on. Have a nice evening." Then he made his way past Harvey towards the door to the service stairwell. He swiped his card, shoved the door open, and looked back at Harvey once more before letting the door close behind him.

"Are you alone now?" asked Melody over the comms.

"Yeah," he replied softly, being careful to look normal. He began a casual stroll to the centre of the large room. "You think your guard is in on it?" he asked.

A few seconds passed before Melody replied. She would be doing what Harvey was doing, playing the role of a security guard's first night at the gallery and pretending to look at the paintings.

"No," she replied. "Too weak, too eager, and too much of a pussy. How about yours?"

"One hundred percent," Harvey replied. "Small time villain caught up with the big boys. Even if he gets away with this, he'll be behind bars in under six months."

"You get his name?"

"No, I caught his breath," said Harvey, stopping to look at a portrait of someone of some significance in a time long passed. "He's Spanish, lazy and arrogant."

"You think he'll be alone?" asked Melody. "Have you seen the painting? It's huge. Far too big for one man to steal."

"The one by the balcony?"

"Yeah, you can't miss it."

Harvey turned back and continued his casual stroll to the balcony where he'd spoken to the guard.

"Are you there?" asked Melody.

"I'm looking at the painting."

"Big, isn't it?" said Melody. "How would you go about stealing that?"

Harvey ran his eyes along the huge, ornately decorated brass frame. A series of small electrical wires ran around the edge of the frame and then joined to run up to the ceiling where, presumably, a series of eyebolts had been drilled in to hold it on the wall. When the painting underwent maintenance, Harvey thought, it had to be removed and lowered to the floor.

"I'm no art thief, Melody," said Harvey, taking in the sheer size of the painting, "but I'd say that stealing this is almost impossible. Get hold of Reg and ask him how much it weighs."

"I've been here all along," said Reg's voice, distant and broken. "Your earpieces are connected via satellite."

"So what does it weigh?"

"Well," began Reg, clearly loving the research, "given the frame's size and thickness, plus it's made from brass, so..." He began to mumble to himself as he ran the calculations in his head.

"Reg?" said Harvey, interrupting the genius calculations. "Just give us a rough idea. We don't need the exact weight."

"Oh, well," he replied, a little discouraged by using rough estimates as opposed to fact, "about half a ton."

"Half a ton?" said Melody. "It's a painting."

"It's solid brass and mounted on a hardwood backboard. And it's the size of my flat in Clapham," said Reg, defending his estimation.

"Harvey, I've got a bad feeling about this," said Melody.

"Agreed."

"I think this is a setup," she continued.

Harvey didn't reply. The sound of heavy boots running up the stairs behind the service door caught his attention. He glanced down and saw Melody. He pointed with one hand to the door she'd used and with the other, he cupped his ear.

Catching on immediately, Melody tucked herself flat against the wall and edged closer to the door.

Three long steps took Harvey to the first-floor service exit. He positioned himself in front of the door, feet planted, and waited.

The seconds passed slowly.

"Hear anything?" he whispered.

"There's someone in the stairwell," replied Melody. "They're counting down for something."

Click. The magnetic lock released.

CHAPTER SEVENTEEN

"Rosa and Diego are in position," announced Antonio. He cupped his hand over the hands-free earpiece connected to his phone and squinted, listening for what Lola presumed to be Rosa giving him an update. "The control room is down, and I have access to the security interface."

Lola watched with admiration as the slight man navigated through the various security prompts. He ran a small program Lola had seen Fingers use before to break the passwords of firewalls. Within moments, Antonio had three windows open on his laptop: the alarms, the cameras and the sensors.

"I'm ready, Dante," he said with practiced calm. "Say the word and I'll kill the alarms."

"Disable the sensors first," said Dante. "In the floor and behind the paintings."

A few deft keystrokes from Antonio and Lola saw the green sensor icons blink to red. A flashing warning began at the top of the screen.

"Good," said Dante. "Leave the cameras on. I want to see this."

He turned to Lola.

"You should watch too, my dear. You might learn a thing or two."

Lola glanced past Dante into the tunnel ahead.

"I wouldn't even think about running," said Dante, catching the movements in her eyes. He nodded to Marco who was standing beside Lola, and she felt his grip on her arm tighten.

"Who are the guards I see?" asked Dante to Antonio.

"Just guards. They'll need to take them out first with the tear gas," replied Antonio.

Dante checked his watch once more. Lola noted the diamond-studded bezel and leather strap.

"Okay, give her the green light. Let's do this," said Dante.

"Rosa, you are go on my count of three," Antonio announced over the comms.

The five of them looked on as if they were watching a football game on the screen. But something was wrong. Lola saw the guard on the ground floor jump to the wall beside the door, and the guard on the first floor moved to stand in front of the first-floor exit.

Dante smiled and gave Lola a sideways glance.

"You recognise them?"

She shook her head.

"They're your father's people. Look how prepared they are. Look how confident they seem. Ready to foil my plans."

It was only when Dante had said the words that Lola became very aware of the guards. It was Harvey and Melody.

Dante gave a laugh.

"Always one step behind. Poor old Smokey. He never learns."

Antonio reached the end of his count. The doors to the ground floor and first-floor service stairwells burst open and chaos played out in black and white across two screens.

Lola struggled to focus, switching between the action on the first floor and the ground floor.

A woman, who Lola assumed to be Rosa, burst through the ground floor exit and tossed a can of tear gas in front of her. She pulled a gas mask down over her face just as the canister gave off a small explosion, bright white on the small black-and-white screen. But Rosa was caught off guard by Melody, who reached out from beside the door, twisted her arm and performed what looked like some kind of judo roll to bring Rosa down. Rosa fought back, and the two women rolled off towards the main entrance as great plumes of thick smoke began to emanate from the canister.

The fighting women rolled to a stop. Lola was surprised to feel pleased that Melody had Rosa pinned to the ground with her knees on her shoulders. But the pleasure in seeing Rosa taken down was replaced with dread as the cloud of smoke washed over them both, shielding them from the cameras.

Upstairs, the camera was aimed at the top of the stairwell and the service exit Diego had burst through. Smoke billowed out from somewhere to the right, off screen. But neither of the two men could be seen. Lola, Dumas, Marco, Luca and Antonio watched the laptop, transfixed and waiting for some kind of movement.

"Get us another view," Dante snapped at Antonio.

He flicked through the cameras, but each of them showed a different angle of a large, empty, rectangular-shaped room with a stairwell at one end and walls lined with paintings. The canister expired, the smoke dwindled to nothing and the view of the empty room began to clear.

Antonio continued to switch cameras, seeking the men. He then flinched; the screen was filled with the face of a man staring into the camera through the protective gas mask. The smoke was clearing fast. When the view had become clear, Lola saw the man was wearing a guard's uniform.

He moved his face close to the camera, peering up and cocking his head as if intrigued. Then he raised a hand and pulled at the mask. Breaking the rubber seal from his skin, he lifted it clear to reveal wild, primal eyes staring into the camera.

"Who is this?" said Dante.

But nobody replied. They were all captivated by Harvey as he bent out of sight and began to drag Diego into view until the screen was filled with just Diego's face.

"You know him?" asked Dante.

But Lola remained silent. She watched as Harvey's two hands held Diego's head from behind. Diego's eyes were wide with fear and red from the gas. Tears streamed down his face, and even on the poor quality camera, they could see the red veins across the whites of his eyes from the gas attack.

His head began to turn to one side, then further. Harvey's firm hands gripped Diego's head. He forced the head to the right as far as he could, against the will of the muscle and sinew that stuck out from Diego's neck and until he was looking back over his right shoulder. Then with a movement so sudden and sharp that Lola gasped in surprise, Harvey ripped Diego's head the opposite way, snapping his neck in one easy, effortless movement.

Diego's head hung, limp and lifeless, for a moment. He fell from the screen, discarded by Harvey who then stepped back into view.

He peered into the lens with eyes as cold as stone.

"I said who is that?" shouted Dante, then backhanded Lola.

"You won't stop him. He's a monster," Lola spat, as she dabbed her lip for signs of blood. "And he'll come for you next. You wait."

Dante took a step towards Lola.

"You think I care about some piece of crap like Diego? Honestly?" he said, his voice quiet and controlled. "Are you really as stupid as your father? Do you think that I would steal the Defeat of the Floating Batteries at Gibraltar?"

"So why send them? Why plan all this?" asked Lola. Her voice, louder than before, echoed through the tiled tunnel.

"You know the trouble with your father, Lola?"

Lola remained silent.

"He has no foresight. He has such visions of grandeur that he can't see past logic. The Defeat of the Floating Batteries is seven metres long and five metres high, Lola. What would even I do with a painting of such a size?"

He turned away and began to pace along the services corridor.

"Rosa is nothing but trouble. She was destined to fail. Her cousin, Diego, was an ignorant pig who deserved to die. And your father's little pets are now trapped."

Lola stared back at him.

"Trapped?"

"Antonio," said Dante, "sound the alarms. It is time for us to go."

CHAPTER EIGHTEEN

The pounding of her heart was intense. Rosa had never felt it beat so hard. She fought to suck air through the restrictive mask, but the claustrophobic feeling was overwhelming. The woman's knees had Rosa pinned to the floor, but her grip on Rosa's neck was waning as the burn began to take effect and the woman's eyes reddened and began to stream.

Soon, her hands released completely. Unable to hold on any longer, she pulled her shirt up to her face and covered her mouth. But it was too late. The effects of the CS gas had already taken hold.

Just then, a piercing whistle rang through the gallery. Spinning orange lights danced off the ceiling and walls. The noise was deafening, and amidst the smoke, the lights were chaotic.

A series of metallic thuds boomed around the room as the slam doors came crashing into place, blocking the exits and windows.

With a sharp twist of her hips, Rosa flicked the woman off and scrambled to her feet, but whatever her misgivings, the woman still had some fight left. Her hand reached out as Rosa stood up, grabbed her belt, and pulled her back down so they were face to face. The effort was futile. Even as she held her there, her burning eyes prevented any follow-up attack. A hard jab from Rosa's elbow to the woman's face easily released the grip. She stepped over the woman, who had curled into a ball covering her face.

Rosa delivered a hard kick to her face.

But the move was blocked, and once more, a hand caught hold of her ankle, twisted and pulled. Rosa toppled. She tried to kick out again, but she went down, only for the woman to clamber on top of her back. The mask was wrenched from her face, pulling Rosa's head back at an unnatural angle. Rosa retaliated by reaching up for the woman's hair and pulling it down hard, until the two women lay side by side. The assailant tried desperately to pull the mask from Rosa, who with one hand held the mask on and with the other landed two hard punches to the woman's face.

Regaining her breath through the restrictive mask took a few seconds, but as Rosa began to stand to move away from the woman, she felt a hand on her belt. Another grabbed her collar. But before she could react, she was hoisted from the floor high into the air.

She screamed at whoever it was to put her down, kicking out with her legs. But he was moving and gaining speed. Then he launched her.

There was a moment of nothing, brief and filled with anxiety, as the tiny parts of her ear deciphered which way was up and which was down.

But the feeling was short-lived.

Rosa slammed into the inner glass doors. The sound of breaking glass and splintering wood was lost against the piercing wail of the alarm. Rosa rolled to a stop on the granite entrance floor. There was no time to assess the damage to her body. Even through the mask, her peripheral caught the movement of the man as he stepped up beside her.

Rosa jumped to her knees, scrambling for a weapon amongst the broken glass. Her hand found a piece, nine-inches long with a sharp point on one end.

She slashed out at his legs as he drew close, and at his hands as he attacked. But he was fast, and trained, judging by the way he moved. Calculated blows from his legs and fists were met with deft swipes of Rosa's weapon. Warm sticky blood dripped from her hand, forcing her to hold the slippery shard of glass tighter. It was her only hope.

But then, as if a whistle had called an end to the bout, he stood up straight then stepped back out of view, leaving Rosa breathless and leaning against the outer glass doors, behind which, the steely slam doors blocked the exit.

"Antonio," she said, "the slam doors are down. Get them up. I'm trapped here."

But Antonio offered no reply.

The man stepped back into view, emerging from the smoke like some kind of apparition.

"Antonio, raise the slam doors, god damn it," she shouted with her finger on her comms.

But it was too late. The man was standing over her, a bright red fire extinguisher held high above his head.

"No," she screamed.

But her scream was cut off as the heavy canister smashed into her body. A rib broke, of that she was sure, and maybe her arm as well. She let go of the glass shard, letting it drop to the floor as the fire extinguisher rolled away.

"Reg," he said, "it's a trap. Get us out of here."

Rosa backed into the corner. The movement crippled her with pain. He was talking to someone. He had outside help.

The slam doors began to rise, slow, mechanical and reluctant. The screaming alarm ceased and the spinning orange lights flicked off.

Outside in the distance, sirens blared, growing closer with each wail.

With an almost animal strength, be reached down and grabbed Rosa's belt. She tried to fight him off. But each blow she delivered stabbed at her ribs, rendering her attack futile.

He lifted her high in the air once more,

turned, and, as the last of the slam door disappeared out of sight, he launched her through the outer doors. Once more, shattering glass slashed at her body. It tore the mask from her head and she hit the cold pavement outside, sliding on her face far enough to feel the pavement tearing at her skin.

Rosa lay there, unable to move. She heard the crunching of glass beneath his boots and braced herself for the follow-up attack.

But it didn't come.

She rolled onto her back, opened her eyes and looked up into his cold stare. He was carrying the girl, and he studied Rosa's face as if committing it to memory. Then as the sirens closed in just a few streets away, he slipped from view.

CHAPTER NINETEEN

Nausea came in waves, washing over Melody and leaving a cold sweat on her skin. Her eyes had stopped streaming and she could focus, but they were sore as if sand lined the inside of her eyelids. She rocked from side to side as Harvey took long fast strides with her in the crook of his arms. Resting her head on his chest, she pulled her arms around him, listening to the calm beat of Harvey's heart. It was as if he was walking in the park on a Sunday afternoon, despite her weight, despite the adrenaline and despite the pace of their escape.

Somewhere in the distance, a swirling mass of sirens silenced.

"I can walk if you want," she offered.

"Can you see?"

"Enough, if you help me."

Melody had always admired how gentle Harvey could be. He was a man known for his violence and brutality, yet with her, he had the softest touch. He lowered her to the ground where Melody felt the cool, soft grass beneath her.

"Where are we?" she whispered, as he leaned across to move her hair and wipe the tears from her eyes.

In the black and blurry night, Harvey was just a shape, dark against an already dark sky.

"In a park. We're safe here," he replied. "Open your eyes and tilt your head."

Cool fresh water ran across her left eye.

"Blink," said Harvey. "Let the water wash the chemicals out."

"What do you think happened?" asked Melody. She tilted her head to the right for Harvey to wash her other eye.

"We were set up."

"What for? Dumas doesn't have the painting. He failed."

"Hold still," said Harvey, as he poured the

remains of the bottle into her eye. "There were only two of them. Not five."

"So?" said Melody.

"So if Dumas wanted the painting as much as Smokey does, he'd have been there himself. And he'd be armed with more than just tear gas," said Harvey.

Shifting her position, Melody rested her head on Harvey's knee.

"So now we've lost Dumas, and we don't have Lola," said Melody. "Sounds like we all lost tonight."

"No," said Harvey, "the game is still on. Dumas is still out there, and my guess is that he's got Lola with him. Whoever they were back there in the gallery were also set up."

"What makes you say that?" asked Melody.

"They had back up. What was the name of Dumas' tech guy?"

"Antonio or something."

"That's him. The girl back there told him to raise the slam doors, but she got no response. It was like she was meant to be trapped there with us."

"But I still don't understand," said Melody.

"If Dumas doesn't want the painting, what does he want?"

"The painting was bait. He knew Smokey would protect it. And by doing so, Dumas knew that Smokey would commit his resources, leaving him free to hit somewhere else."

"Something bigger?"

"Bigger than a seven-metre painting?" said Harvey.

"More valuable, at least," replied Melody. "So how do we find him?"

"We need to find Lola," said Harvey. He hit the button on his earpiece.

"Reg, come back."

"I was wondering how you two were getting on. I've got eyes on the gallery. It's swarmed with police. They've got the girl, and they found a body."

"No sign of Dumas then?" said Melody, who opened the channel on her own earpiece.

"No sign of Dumas. Just a control room full of dead guards, one dead criminal and a half-dead girl laying on the pavement outside. How are your eyes?"

"Better. Still sore, but it could have been worse."

"Reg, it's Harvey. We need to find Lola. Where was her last known location?"

They heard Reg's fingers scrambling across his keyboard and his under-the-breath mutterings as he spoke to himself while he worked.

In the reprise, Melody managed to catch Harvey's eye. It wasn't much, but it was enough for her to see that inside him, somewhere buried deep down, there was a chance that he felt the same as she did.

"Righto," said Reg. "I've found her phone. It looks like it's in a side street near Cannon Street Station."

"We can walk that from here," said Harvey.

"I'm sending you the location now," said Reg. "Do you guys need anything else?"

"Yes," said Melody. "We don't think Dumas wanted the painting after all."

"So why go to all the effort?"

"It was a trap, a trap Dumas knew Smokey would fall for. From now on, we call the shots."

"Copy that," said Reg.

"The painting was a decoy. Even Cordero thought Dumas would be there. See if you can find something else that Dumas might want to steal."

"Something else?" said Reg. "You mean you want me to find expensive pieces of art in London? I imagine fifty percent of privately-owned art is in this city."

"Not London as a whole, Reg. The City. It needs to be in the City. You say Lola was last seen near Cannon Street? Start there. It's a twenty-minute walk from here, so have some answers ready."

"Gotcha," said Reg, sounding enthused by the call for research.

Harvey clicked off his comms. Melody followed suit.

"We're on our own now," she said, pulling his hand to her face and holding it against her skin.

"Melody," said Harvey.

"Don't," she replied, savouring the feel of him. "I've missed this."

"Melody," he said again. But Melody ignored him and rolled closer.

A dog barked somewhere close by and the trample of heavy boots on concrete were loud in the quiet night.

Without warning, Harvey scrambled to his feet and pulled Melody up by her arms. "We have to go," he said. "Now."

CHAPTER TWENTY

Harvey pulled Melody to her feet and dragged her across the grass to the wrought-iron gate on the edge of the little park in London Moorgate.

Melody seemed confused at first, but when she heard the clicking of the German Shepherd's paws on the footpath, she caught on and ran alongside Harvey. A taxi rolled by. It slowed as if the driver was hoping for a fare then drove on when Harvey turned his back on the driver to face the oncoming dog.

"Stop," said Harvey, planting his feet and pulling Melody behind him. The dog's speed increased as it drew closer.

"Harvey, what are you doing?" asked

Melody, sliding behind him. "Let's get out of here."

But Harvey kept his ground in the centre of the small, empty road that ran around the park.

"We'll never outrun it," he replied quietly. "Trust me."

He made eye contact with the dog at twenty metres, which at first seemed to aggravate the animal. But as the distance closed and Harvey held his ground, the dog slowed. Its tail dropped low and the hackles on its back flattened.

The large, eighty-pound German Shepherd came to an abrupt stop at Harvey's feet. He sniffed at his legs once then sat and held Harvey's stare, its ears flat against its head. Melody took a step back from Harvey and the dog growled once. But one look back at Harvey and the dog quietened.

"Harvey, I hope you know what you're doing."

The boots Harvey had heard in the park emerged from the iron gates as a six-foot-something policeman with a bright yellow jacket came running after the dog.

"Stop right there," he called to Harvey.

The dog turned its head to its master, then returned its attention to Harvey.

"Bruno, attack."

But the dog remained still even as the policeman approached.

"Oh for god's sake, Harvey," Melody muttered under her breath. "That's it now."

"Do you mind telling me why you're running, sir?" asked the policeman, panting as he approached.

Harvey didn't reply.

The policeman raised his hand to operate his shoulder-mounted radio.

"I wouldn't do that," said Harvey.

The policeman stopped.

"Is that right? And why is that?" he asked.

"Let go of the radio, officer."

"I'm going to need to take your name, sir," he continued. He spoke into his radio. "Control three two four. Control three two four. I have the suspect."

"I said let go of the radio."

"Right, sir, you leave me no option. Put your hands behind your back. You too, miss." The officer reached for his handcuffs but the sudden action triggered the dog's defensive nature; he turned and growled at his owner.

"Why don't you put your hands where I can see them?" said Harvey.

"Bruno?"

The dog continued to growl. His upper lip upturned and the hackles raised on his nape.

"Hands," said Harvey.

In a smooth, slow motion, the officer brought his hands to his front. In one hand was a pair of matte black handcuffs.

"Why don't you put them on?" said Harvey.

"Oh my god," said Melody from behind him. "You can't be doing this."

The houses at the end of the dark street lit up with the flashing blues of an approaching squad car.

"Do it fast," said Harvey.

The dog continued to growl at its handler as the cuffs clicked into place.

Harvey reached out, with one eye on the dog, and unclipped the radio from the policeman's belt. Then he pulled the push-to-talk unit from the man's shoulder.

"Let's go," said Melody. She knew not to mention Harvey's name.

But Harvey didn't move. The flashing

blues drew closer behind the line of trees that bordered the park.

"You won't get away with this," said the officer.

As Harvey checked to see how close the car was, the officer pulled his telescopic cosh from his belt. In an instant, the dog leapt up at the man, biting down hard on his arm and using all of his weight to pull the man to the ground.

"Now let's move," said Harvey, taking Melody's wrist.

He turned and walked away into Moorgate with Melody behind him. They slipped into a late night pub as the blue lights lit the street behind them.

A rowdy crowd of four men in jeans and construction boots were standing at the far end of the bar and eyed them both as they bustled in. Their eyes hovered on Melody's tight jacket and her red, swollen eyes until Harvey pulled her past them towards the rear exit.

Four heads turned. Harvey ignored them.

The door to the washroom opened, blocking his way. A large man in light blue jeans, a white t-shirt and tan steel-toed boots stepped out. He was taller than Harvey by a clear four inches. At first, he apologised and moved to one side to allow the pair through, but when he caught sight of Melody's swollen eyes, his arm reached across the narrow hallway and blocked Harvey once more.

"Are you okay there, sweetheart?" he asked Melody, his Irish accent thick and fast.

"She's fine, mate. Move out the way, eh?" said Harvey, aware of the flashing blues that shone through the windows, rhythmically lighting the inside of the bar.

"I didn't ask you, sunshine. I was talking to the lady." He turned back to Melody. "Is he giving you bother?"

With a roll of her eyes and a glance at the blue lights in the mirrors behind the bar, Melody shook her head.

"No," she said. "It's fine. We need to go."

But the man caught the flash of blue, then studied them both, putting two and two together.

"Are they for you?" he asked, and gestured at the lights. "Have you got yourselves into a spot of bother, eh?"

"Mate, do yourself a favour," began Harvey, "move out the way. Sit down with your mates and forget you ever saw us. It'll be better for everyone."

The man laughed in Harvey's face. A few hours of drinking beer had soured his breath and the stench of his body odour added to the mix.

"Or what?"

He turned to block their path.

CHAPTER TWENTY-ONE

"What the bloody hell just happened?" shouted Dumas. His voice seemed to run along the tiled tunnel and return to Lola in a haunted whisper.

Nobody spoke.

"Somebody answer me," Dumas shouted.

"They got away, boss," said Antonio.

"They got away?" repeated Dumas. "How did they get away? I thought you were the one controlling the doors?"

"I am, but they must have access too."

"So how can they open the doors if you are the one controlling them?"

"I-I-," Antonio began to stammer.

"It's rhetorical, Antonio. Now tell me where they went."

"I-I-," Antonio began to stammer again.

"Find them," shouted Dumas. Then he turned to Lola. "Who are they? You know them. You must do. Of course, you do. Tell me who they are."

But before Lola could answer, Dumas returned his attention to Antonio, whose hands shook as they hammered the keyboard. Various windows popped up on the screen.

"You have found them?" spat Dumas, his Spanish accent strengthening with his anger.

"I'm trying to access the security cameras in the area," replied Antonio.

"Try harder," said Dumas.

Then once more, he shifted to Lola.

"Do you think it really matters?" he asked. "You think that just because your friends escaped that they will find us here and stop us?" He shook his head. "No. Because, like I said, your father is very short-sighted. It would have been nice if your friends would have been trapped, and your father would have been implicated. He should have gone to prison a long time ago, Lola, but with his silver tongue and his money, he has managed to avoid it. Like the snake, he basks in the sunlight then slivers away under his rock when the heat gets too much."

"You're wrong if you think I'm going to stand here and defend him, Dumas," said Lola. "And you're wrong if you think I know anything about any of this. What my father does is his business. What I do is my business. We're two people. Two minds. Do not paint me with the same poisoned brush you use on my father."

Dumas considered Lola's statement. He turned and strode away in five slow, methodical steps. He swivelled on his feet, took the same five slow, methodical steps back to Lola and slapped her hard across the face.

"You're right. You are two people. But inside you runs your father's blood. It courses through your veins, Lola. Your father taught you well. I know he did. I have been watching from afar. A spectator of your career. Do you wonder why I have brought you here to this place, so far underground?"

"Because you're insane?"

Dumas laughed.

"No, Lola. It is because your father's blood runs through your veins. You saw the lengths your father would go to protect The Defeat of the Floating Batteries at Gibraltar. I imagine your friends would require fake security, they would have floor-plans of the gallery, and they clearly had access to the security cameras. All of these things require resources, Lola. Your father's resources."

"So?" said Lola, still licking the blood from her lip.

"So, imagine if your father had a choice. Where would his loyalty lie? With the arts? Or with his beloved daughter?"

Lola remained quiet. It was a question she'd asked herself before, but she'd never found an answer. A swell of tears, anger and frustration grew behind her eyes, hot and pulsing with the beat of her heart.

"Mark my words, Lola, before the night is out, your father will show his face." He stepped closer to Lola and held a strand of her hair between two fingers. He sniffed at it, his eyes closed to savour the smell. Then he let go of her hair and let his face take on a cold, remorseless stare. "Or he will lose his daughter."

"I have found them," announced Antonio. "They are inside this bar here. Look."

Dumas glanced across at the laptop that Antonio was presenting.

"Good work," he said. "Are you sure it's them?"

"Positive. I will never forget that man's eyes," said Antonio.

"Good. Tip the police off. Let's make sure they do not scupper our plans."

CHAPTER TWENTY-TWO

Four wooden stools scraped across the old, wooden floor. Four large shapes closed the way behind Harvey and Melody. The large man in front smiled.

"I don't like bullies," he said. His eyes flicked to Melody and back to Harvey.

"This is your last chance," Harvey replied. "Sit down with your mates. Forget you ever saw me." But the sentiment was lost on the man, who looked down on Harvey with disgust. "Melody, go take a seat at the bar. Keep an eye on the door. Order these men five large whiskeys and five bags of ice."

Melody edged past the men as the man in front of Harvey erupted.

"You can't buy your way out of this, sunshine. The way I see it, you have two choices. You can lay on the floor and let us kick the living hell out of you. Or, I'll knock you down, and then we'll kick the living hell out of you."

Harvey was standing in a narrow hallway. If he stretched his arms out, he could touch both walls. Photographs of London from the early nineteen hundreds lined the walls to the washrooms in cheap frames that each shielded their own square of clean paintwork in the surrounding walls stained with a hundred-year-old layer of dirt and tobacco.

Harvey rolled his neck, waiting for the satisfying click each side.

Behind the man in front was the rear exit, which Harvey guessed would lead to an alleyway or beer garden. Either way, it would be a route out of there that wouldn't be covered by City of London security cameras. The wooden door had nine small opaque windows arranged three by three. The reflection of the men behind Harvey was distorted but clear enough. The men were standing two by two like ranks waiting for the command to step into battle.

"Who's first?" asked Harvey.

He hadn't finished his sentence when the big man jabbed out at Harvey's face. It was a move Harvey was ready for. He cocked his head to one side, reached up with his right hand and twisted the man's arm back. Using the momentum of the punch, Harvey pulled his attacker towards him, kicked down sideways on his knee and delivered a finishing blow to the man's throat.

Harvey dropped the big man to the floor wheezing for breath and clutching his ruined leg with gritted teeth. Then he turned to face the four behind him.

He studied the men for a second.

"You're a lefty, you're a righty," he said to the front two. "You're fat, and you're ugly," he finished, addressing the rear two with his last comments.

The two men in front were shorter than the two behind but stocky from a life of construction work. Before either man could react, Harvey took a stride forwards and slammed his forehead into lefty's nose. As if on cue, righty took a wild untrained swing at Harvey who pulled the still-stunned lefty into the line of fire. The man's punch connected with his friend and Harvey shoved the limp body towards righty, who instinctively caught him then, realising his mistake, dropped him. But it was too late. The second it had taken for him to catch his friend had been long enough for Harvey to grab his throat, pinch his windpipe and deliver three hard jabs to his stomach, the last of which cracked a rib.

Righty fell to his knees alongside his two friends, fighting for breath.

Harvey turned to face the remaining two Irishmen.

Ugly took a step forwards, ducking through the doorway into the narrow hall, but all Harvey had to do was to stamp on his outstretched leg as he did, and the man was down.

"Just you left, fatty," said Harvey. "Fancy your chances?"

The last man was left standing alone, dumbfounded at what had just taken place. In less than ten-seconds, his friends had all been floored. A forced look of feigned anger appeared on his face as if he might scare Harvey into reconsidering his position. But Harvey remained firm.

Then, from nowhere, the sound of glass shattering broke the silence. A boot swung up from behind and crunched between the fat man's legs. Fatty fell to his knees, revealing Melody who was standing behind him. She kicked him out of the way and ran past Harvey to the rear door.

"Let's go, Harvey. I couldn't let you have all the fun, could I?" she said with a smile. Then she pulled the door open and checked outside just as the front door to the bar crashed open.

CHAPTER TWENTY-THREE

There was no time to be selective. The inside of the pub had hushed when Harvey and the men had fought, but when the front doors were kicked open and armed police stormed inside, the place erupted. Melody scrambled over the outside side wall with Harvey on her heels. Shouts boomed from behind them as they sought an exit through the neighbouring property.

"Reg, we're going to need your help here," said Melody, pushing the button on her earpiece.

As faithful as a hound, Reg swung into action.

"Let's see where you are," he began.

Melody pictured him staring at his screen and working with his homemade software, LUCY, a program designed to track people, phones and tap into satellites to provide live views anywhere in the world.

"No time for fancy games, Reg. We just need an out and fast," said Harvey.

"Okay, I found you. There's a courtyard to the rear of the next property, and behind that is an alleyway that'll take you back onto the main street. I'm on the live satellite now and you have a clear run out. I'd suggest heading north and getting out of there. The place is heating up fast."

Both Harvey and Melody scaled the wall and dropped into the courtyard of an office building. They saw the narrow pass between the two buildings and slipped onto Queen Victoria Street.

"Hey guys," said Reg, "I said to head north. You're going south-east."

Harvey grabbed Melody's hand and walked casually across the road into a smaller lane as if they were just an ordinary couple strolling home from work.

"No time, Reg," said Harvey. "We need to find Lola. We're heading for Cannon

Street Station. Have you found Dumas' target?"

"There's so much art in the City. Dumas could be going after any of it. We have no way of knowing," said Reg.

"What does Smokey have to say about it?" asked Melody.

"Not a lot. Now he knows the painting is safe, I think the reality that his daughter has been kidnapped has hit home. He went back up to the main house feeling unwell."

"Reg, we're five minutes from Cannon Street. Find Dumas," said Harvey, then switched off his comms.

Behind them on the main road, a convoy of police cars raced past with their sirens blaring. Melody turned to see the last of them slow, then stop.

It began to turn.

"Harvey," she said, "we've got company."

"Don't look," he replied. He held her hand and crossed the street into another side street. Once out of view of the police, they both ran. The buildings either side of the narrow cobbled street channelled the noise of the engine as the driver gave chase.

Harvey tugged Melody through alleyways, left then right, until they found them-selves on the pedestrianised pathway beside the River Thames. London Bridge was ahead. A few drunken office workers stumbled to-wards them as they ran. Melody didn't need to turn to look; they could hear the pounding of heavy boots behind them.

A ramp leading up to the bridge and Lower Thames Street came up on their right, so they took it then ran with everything they had. Sirens were growing louder as more po-lice were called in to close them off. They reached Lower Thames Street at a set of traffic lights. To their right, coming from the Tower of London, three police cars sped into view. To their left, another set of flashing blues waited for them.

"We're trapped," said Melody, as they reached the road. Behind them, two po-licemen chasing on foot had just turned the corner.

Before Melody could stop him, Harvey stepped out into the busy road. A taxi swerved to miss him and slammed into the car in the next lane in a hiss of angry steam. The two cars ground to a halt. Two more cars failed to stop in time and smashed into the back end of them, forcing the crash onwards. A motorbike slowed and swerved to avoid the crash, but the rider turned too fast and slid off. The bike came to a halt a few feet in front of Harvey, who picked it up, swung his leg over, revved the engine and shouted to Melody.

"Get on, now."

"What the bloody hell are you doing?" she shouted back at him as she climbed on. Harvey dropped the bike into first gear, revved once more and tore away from the scene.

Harvey didn't reply.

The police car that had been waiting for them roared into life, blocking their way. Harvey mounted the pavement, ducked beneath a traffic sign and took the bike down to the riverside pathway where the cars couldn't follow.

"Reg, we need some help here," said Melody. She switched her comms to open then pulled her arm around Harvey again.

"What the hell are you guys up to?" replied Reg.

"Getting away," said Melody. "Have you found Dumas yet?"

"No," replied Reg, "there's just too many options."

"Where are we heading, Reg?" she shouted above the noise of the motorbike's engine as Harvey slowed to take the bike onto a tiny side street called Swan Lane, back towards the city.

"Cannon Street Station," said Reg. "There's a van parked down a side street, Bush Lane. I'm pretty sure that's where Lola's phone signal came from. Right now, you're four hundred yards away."

"Four hundred yards. Bush Lane down the side of Cannon Street Station," she called to Harvey. Then she returned her attention to Reg. "Hey, Reg, we're coming in hot. Is there anything you can do to help us out here?"

She heard the clatter of keys once more as Reg looked at his options.

"Hold on," he replied. "I've got an idea."

CHAPTER TWENTY-FOUR

"They got away, Dante," said Antonio. "The police haven't found them."

Dumas took three angered steps toward Antonio, stared at the screen and saw the police walking out empty-handed as two EMTs walked into the pub, their ambulance parked a few metres away.

"Are you sure it was them that went inside?" asked Dumas.

"Positive," replied Antonio. "Why else would there be an ambulance on the scene?"

"Can you see where they went?" asked Dumas.

"I'm trying now," replied Antonio, as he flicked between CCTV cameras and began muttering to himself, just as Lola had seen Fingers do whenever he was deep inside a security system. "They could only have gone out the back, which means they could only come out here, here or here."

Each of the various CCTV screens flashed up for a second and were then replaced by the next.

"Here," he cried out. "I have them walking away further down the street. The stupid police are not even looking."

"Well, why don't we hold off phase two of our plan? Maybe we can kill two birds with one stone, if you pardon the pun."

Dumas smiled a cruel smile, which was mirrored by Luca and Marco.

"What's phase two?" asked Lola.

But Dumas just laughed at the question and turned his attention to Antonio.

"See if you can draw them in and make sure we have a good view. I don't want to miss this."

"They're near the river," said Antonio. "How about if I send a little alert to the emergency services?" His fingers played across the keys, and Lola watched with despair as a convoy of police cars cruised

Lower Thames Street just moments away from Harvey.

The last car stopped beside the entrance to the side street where Harvey and Melody had disappeared.

It turned.

While Antonio flicked through the metropolitan police CCTV software searching for the right camera, Dumas turned back to Lola to gauge her reaction.

Lola remained impassive.

"Do you gamble, Lola?" he asked.

"Every time I cross the street," she replied.

Dumas dismissed the comment with a smile.

"If I were a gambling man, I would say that your father's friends are in a lot of trouble. But who will get them first? The police?" His mannerisms turned dramatic. "Or me?"

"I would say neither. The police will catch you. At least, you better hope they do."

"And what do you mean by that?"

"Well, Dante, if the police catch you, they might rough you up a little. You'll go to prison, but I imagine you're a fast learner. You'll survive."

"But?" Dumas prompted.

"If he gets you..." Lola nodded at Harvey's form on the screen. "You'll be in a whole world of hurt."

"So you do know him? Do I sense a hint of admiration in your voice?" said Dumas. He flicked his eyes up at Marco who reached from behind her with both hands, pinching her windpipe with one hand and her nose with the other.

Lola fought back, kicking and squirming, but Marco's grip was strong.

Dumas nodded once more at Marco, and his grip loosened but still held her tight.

"Tell me who he is," said Dumas.

Lola sucked in huge lungfuls of air, coughed and composed herself.

"If there's one person in this world who you should be afraid of, it's him. If there's one person who can stop you, it's him."

"I need a name, Lola," said Dumas. Once more, he flicked a nod at Marco and the suffocation began again.

But Lola was ready for the attack. She flung her head back and connected with Marco's nose. Then she spun and kicked out at his legs before landing a hard punch to his throat.

Before Marco had a chance to react, Luca

reached across and with one hand grabbed Lola's throat and slammed her into the tiled wall.

Dumas appeared impressed. He smiled his sickening smile and watched as Marco straightened, embarrassed at the blows he'd taken.

"I've got them," said Antonio, disrupting the fight. "They're on a motorbike."

The group all craned to see the action unfold on Antonio's laptop screen. Harvey and Melody were racing from the scene of a crash. A police car blocked their way, but Harvey hopped the bike onto the pavement and tore off towards the river.

"Follow them," demanded Dumas.

"I can do better than that," said Antonio. A fresh window opened on his laptop showing a map of the City of London and icons at each junction.

"What are you doing?" asked Dumas. "I told you to follow them."

"Relax," replied Antonio. "There's only one way out for them." He clicked on one of the icons and another little window opened. "If I click here and here," he said, again muttering to himself, "then the traffic lights will remain red."

Antonio clicked the button to save his changes to the traffic signals. Then he turned to explain. "The City of London is the only city in the UK where the police can override the traffic signals. I can access it from the same console as the security cameras. It's a security feature they built when they created the steel circle."

"You mean the ring of steel?" said Lola.

"Yes, this," said Antonio. "Now, if I give them a green light here," he said, watching on the CCTV screen as Harvey and Melody took Antonio's route, "I can make them dance."

A few moments later, Antonio switched to yet another camera feed and watched as Harvey and Melody's bike stopped in a side street. Parked two hundred yards in front of them was the van that Lola had been thrown into.

Once more, Dumas smiled when he saw her reaction. Her face dropped in horror.

"Before I kill them both," said Dumas, "won't you tell me his name? It'll help me sleep at night."

He glanced back at the screen. Harvey hadn't moved. They were both sitting on the bike staring at the van.

"Tell me," shouted Dumas, and slapped Lola across the face.

The strike reopened the wound from his previous slaps. Lola spat blood on the floor and stared back at him, licking her lip and tasting the iron.

"He's the devil," she said. "And he's coming for you, Dumas."

CHAPTER TWENTY-FIVE

Bush Lane was a typical London side street, narrow, paved with cobblestones and with large buildings on either side. The gaps between the buildings channelled the sounds of London's Metropolitan Police as they searched the surrounding roads.

"Is that it?" asked Harvey. "The silver van?"

"According to the signal," replied Reg. "A word of warning, I've hacked the traffic signals and I'm trying to deflect the police, but it looks like someone else has the same idea."

"You mean Dumas' man?" asked Melody.

"It has to be," said Reg. "The police are closing in. You guys need to move fast."

"Do you think she's inside?" asked Melody.

"Only one way to find out," said Harvey. He made to kick the stand down, but Melody stepped off the bike before him and ran to the side of the building.

"I'll check the van. If the police come around that corner, you take them on a wild goose chase," she called.

Harvey revved the bike once and checked his mirrors while Melody made her way towards the van. She was fifteen metres away when she stopped and glanced back at Harvey, just as the first blue lights rounded the corner.

The driver of the police car slammed the accelerator and the sirens echoed down the lane. Melody stepped back into a doorway as Harvey took off past the van. He rounded a left-hand bend and felt the rear wheel of the bike slip on the uneven surface. But he countered the skid, straightened and took the next right turn into a dead end. The road was blocked with metre-high bollards two metres apart to stop cars using the back street as a shortcut, but the bike skipped through easily.

There was a screech of tyres behind him

as the police cars skidded to a stop, but Harvey was already away on Upper Thames Street looking for a way out of the area. Although it was midnight, the street was crammed with cars honking their horns. Cab drivers were standing beside their taxis to see what was going on ahead, but the traffic lights remained red.

"Reg, can you get me a route out of here?" he asked over the comms.

"I'm working on it," Reg replied.

The left-turn traffic light turned green. Harvey made his way along the right side of the road then, at the last minute, he cut in and joined the traffic heading over Southwark Bridge.

A policeman trying to control the volume of waiting traffic at the junction caught Harvey's manoeuvre and immediately hit his radio while running back to his squad car. A few moments later, while Harvey was tearing across the bridge, blue lights lit up his side mirror.

"Okay, Reg, I need two more things," said Harvey, as he slipped between two cars and out of sight of the police.

"What do you need, Harvey?" said Reg. He was clearly enjoying the buzz of the chase.

"I've got police all over me so I'm going to have to ditch this bike and get back to Melody somehow. Find me a basement car park and fix those traffic lights. It's mayhem back there and I don't need to be sitting in traffic."

"Easy," said Reg. "Take the first right after the bridge. A car park is on your right-hand side. I'm on the CCTV there. It looks like there's a nightclub or a bar or something. Lots of people outside. You can lose yourself in there."

"Nice work, Reg."

"Ah, it's good to have you back, Harvey," replied Reg.

Harvey checked his mirrors. There were three police cars twenty cars behind him. He slowed a little, forcing the car behind him to slow and slam his horn. Then Harvey dropped the bike to the right and shot through a tiny gap in the oncoming traffic. Without even looking behind him for the police, he turned again and slipped around the side of a barrier at the entrance to the underground car park.

At the bottom of the ramp, the car park led around to the left with spaces on both sides and a slope to the next lower level. Harvey revved the engine, found second gear, released the clutch then hopped off the back of the bike, letting it roll on and crash into a parked Ford. Without stopping to look, Harvey ran to a set of glass doors. A magnetic lock was fixed to one side, the type that required a programmed key card to release it.

Harvey strode up to the door and slammed his foot through the glass, which shattered but held in place. Three more kicks pushed the shattered window unit out of the frame, and Harvey slipped through.

The commotion disturbed a security guard, who put his head around the corner and, seeing Harvey, reached for his radio. But it was too late. Before he could even hit the button, Harvey had twisted his arm behind his back, pulled his radio from his epaulette and slammed the guard's head into the wall. He dropped the man where he was standing and made towards the stairs, decommissioning the radio as he walked. He tossed the remains into a wastepaper basket beside the guard's desk on the ground floor, pulled off his jacket and slung it over his shoulder, then stepped out to join the crowd of people standing outside the bar at high tables.

Discreetly, Harvey snatched a bottle of beer from a table where a group of four office workers were standing. He stayed between them and another group of girls while the police wrestled with the car park barrier a few metres away. The barrier raised and all three cars raced down the ramp in convoy.

Harvey returned the beer, thanked the bemused man, and walked to the corner where he hailed a passing cab and climbed inside as two more police cars raced to the scene and closed off the little side street.

"Cannon Street," he said to the driver, offering no please or thanks.

The driver gave a questioning look in the mirror as the mayhem began to erupt behind them. But Harvey just leaned back and looked out of the window. He pulled his phone out of his pocket, pretended to dial a number and put it against his ear.

"Reg, are you there?" he asked.

"Copy that, Harvey," replied Reg over the comms.

"Do you see me?" he asked.

"I'm the only one who does," said Reg.

"Half of London's police force is on its way there."

"Well, hopefully, that'll buy us some time. How's Melody doing?"

"I'm doing fine," said Melody. "The van hasn't moved. No sign of-"

Her voice was suddenly lost to a stream of static.

"Melody, come back," said Harvey.

No reply.

"Reg, I just lost Melody."

"Me too. I've lost everything" replied Reg.

"Is Lola's phone still alive?"

"It is, but I can't get onto it. There's something blocking the signal."

The taxi pulled out of Southwark Bridge Road and onto Upper Thames Street. The roads were still full, but the traffic was returning to normal.

"Melody, come back," Harvey repeated.

No reply.

"Mate, drop me anywhere here," said Harvey, banging the glass behind the driver, with his other hand on the door handle. He stuffed a twenty-pound note from his pocket through the window. "Keep the change. Open the door."

The door lock clicked open, and Harvey burst from the car. He ran across Upper Thames Street between the slow-moving traffic on the far side of the road and onto the pedestrian footpath.

"Reg, keep trying Melody," he shouted as he ran.

A few moments later, he turned at full speed through the metre-high bollards that he'd taken the bike through a short while before. Then he turned again onto Bush Lane.

In his ear, he heard Reg's attempts at getting through to Melody. But all that came back were waves of static.

"The signal's being blocked, Harvey," said Reg.

Harvey took the bend at full pelt, just in time to see Melody step from the doorway, her finger on her ear as if trying to work her earpiece.

With a final burst of energy, Harvey gave everything he had. He tried to call out, but as he opened his mouth to shout her name, a flash of white light split the dark street. A bone-shattering crack followed a fraction of a second later and a ball of flame erupted from the van, blowing the doors and windows across the cobbled street. Glass and broken bricks rained down from the building beside the ruined vehicle and a mushroom cloud of black smoke rose up from the wall of fire.

The blast stopped Harvey dead in his tracks, knocking him off his feet and hurling him backwards. He landed on his back, rolled and covered his face as shards of glass and debris began to hit the cobbled street.

"Melody?" he called, scrambling back to his feet.

Melody didn't reply.

He hobbled closer, his leg bruised from the fall.

"Melody?"

But Melody didn't reply.

"Reg, are you there?"

At first, Reg too failed to respond.

"Reg? Talk to me. Did you see that? Can you see her? I can't see anything down here."

No reply came from Reg. But Harvey could hear the rasp of his breathing, faint and in shock.

"Reg, I need you, mate. Do you have eyes on Melody?"

While Reg composed himself, Harvey limped towards the ruined van. More sirens filled the night and people had started to emerge at the end of the road, like zombies drawn to the burning light. Even from a distance, Harvey could see that two girls had their phones out, recording what they saw.

Thick smoke emanated from the carcass of the van, and as Harvey got closer, a police car pulled in from Cannon Street. Harvey searched the smoke for Melody. He pulled his t-shirt up to his face, squinting his eyes.

"Melody?" he called. But there was no answer.

To his left, the blast had blown through a set of fire doors. One now hung from broken hinges. The other had been completely torn off and lay on the ground. An ambulance followed the police car, and behind that, more police arrived. Using the smoke for cover, Harvey ducked into the destroyed fire exit. But as he stepped through, something caught his eye.

Through the haze of the roaring fire and billowing smoke, behind the silver van lying unmoving on the cold cobbled road, was a body. A police car screeched to a stop beside it.

Harvey lingered, slipping further into the

building but with his eyes fixed on the body. The world about him began to swirl. He reached out, holding onto the wall for balance. Two men in green uniforms crouched either side of the body as firefighters ran by shouting orders.

A stretcher was laid out and the two EMTs coordinated rolling the lifeless body onto it.

Thick wavy hair lay across a bloodied face. The jacket was torn and more blood soaked through from a deep wound in her side. But despite the wounds. Despite the blood.

It was her.

CHAPTER TWENTY-SIX

The CCTV feed showed a black screen. Antonio searched for another camera further from the blast. The silence was broken by Dumas.

"That, my girl, was phase two."

"You're a monster."

"And he was the devil, so you say," said Dumas. "But as you just saw, he was just a man, as mortal as you and I."

Dumas turned and began to walk along the tunnel with renewed energy.

"Let's go," he called. "Phase three."

Antonio quickly disconnected the cable from the laptop, and Marco shoved Lola forwards a little harder than necessary. She glared at him and the two shared a silent game of dare.

"Now. Move," called Dumas from around the long sweeping bend in the tunnel.

They came to a fork. A smaller tunnel branched off left and the larger service tunnel branched off right. Dumas waited for them all to walk into view then began along the left-hand tunnel.

Lola reached up and let her hair down, feigning fatigue. She massaged her head with her fingers, then rolled and rubbed her neck.

"What is this?" she asked. "Where are you taking me?"

"My dear, Lola, do you understand the City of London at all? The security measures that are in place? It's one of the safest and well-equipped cities in Europe, you know. The world, more likely."

"I know enough," replied Lola, leaving room for Dumas to embellish on what he knew along with a clue as to his plans.

"So, you know about the ring of steel. But there's so much more to it than a few po-licemen at strategic places on the City boundary. The City of London has been a target for terrorists for many years. Throughout history, many organisations have put their mark on the City, some more successfully than others."

"So you're a terrorist now?" said Lola. "I thought you were just a greedy art thief like my father?"

"No, Lola, I am no terrorist. But I am a smart man, if I do say so myself. If you know a system well enough, you can manipulate it. You can use it to your advantage. That's all we're doing, using the system to our advantage."

"How do you plan on doing that?"

"Keep walking," said Dumas. "We have a way to go yet."

The tunnel was well lit, an endless length of featureless, tiled walls sweeping left and right.

"What do you think is kept in the City of London?" asked Dumas.

Lola shrugged.

"The banks, some art, probably some stuff no-one knows about."

"There's more than banks and art here, Lola," said Dumas. "Tell me what you think happens when something triggers the security in the city."

"The police swoop in. They close off the

roads, and those cameras you were looking at track whoever did whatever it was that triggered the alarms."

"You're right, but that's only about five percent of what happens. There's a chain reaction. First, the security, as you rightly say, track the target. While this happens, the ring of steel shuts the city down. Nobody gets in, and if the scenario is bad enough, nobody gets out."

"You mean if they think the perpetrator is still inside the ring?"

A cool breeze began to lift Lola's hair from her shoulder.

"Exactly. Then a communication plan feeds through the ranks, up the ladder one rung at a time. The level of severity determines which rung it stops at. Can you guess who's at the top rung?"

"The prime minister?"

"That's right, Lola. Do you remember the terrible bombs a decade ago? Buses and trains were the targets."

"Yeah, seven seven."

"After that episode, the underground system was incorporated into the plans."

They turned a final bend where the white

tiled walls stopped, and before them, running left to right, was a dark and dirty underground tunnel. Below them were three raised tracks that the trains ran on. To their left, a small three-runged ladder reached down onto a small concrete walkway that ran along the side of the dark and gloomy underground.

Luca handed out torches.

"Not far now," said Dumas, offering a tight, satisfied smile. His voice was louder now in the much larger tunnel than before and seemed to roll on and on into the darkness ahead.

"I still can't see how any of that helps you," said Lola.

"Do you hear any trains?" asked Dumas.

"They stop the trains too?"

Dumas smiled.

"Now you're getting there," he said. "This way."

The smell of dust and damp was strong. In the shadows, Lola caught the faint movements of rats scurrying, enjoying the break in train activity and venturing out to scavenge the trash that commuters so often discarded into the tunnel.

"Right about now," Dumas continued, his

voice loud in the tunnel and reverberating off the curved walls in a seemingly endless journey, "thousands of passengers are being evacuated from the underground stations. Protocol dictates that each train stops at the next station and shuts down. Teams of security professionals swoop in, and one by one, they search each and every train. Only once they are all cleared will the service resume."

"You're going to steal a train?" asked Lola.

"In a fashion," said Dumas. "Do you know what is above us right now?"

"The city," said Lola, "and probably thousands of screaming passengers all scared to death."

"And?" said Dumas.

He stopped walking and shone his torchlight on a set of three steps that led up to an old, steel door.

"Above us, Lola, is hope. It is our dreams. And it is everything you could ever wish for. It is my legacy. My birth right."

"Why don't you stop being cryptic and tell me what it is?"

Dumas nodded at Luca, who climbed the few steps and opened the heavy steel door. Two rats ran from the tiny room, squeaking in surprise. They jumped down into the tunnel, ran across Lola's boot and disappeared from view.

"They won't hurt you," said Dumas, seeing Lola's expression.

The door opened into a tiny, lightless room that Lola presumed to be a storage space of some sort. Luca's torch cut beams of light through thick, dusty, stale air. In the left-hand corner was a generator along with a pile of power tools: drills, grinders and saws. The right-hand wall was peppered with drill holes to form a circle eighteen inches in diameter.

"You're breaking into somewhere," said Lola.

"All your dreams, Lola," whispered Dumas from behind her. "Hopes and dreams."

CHAPTER TWENTY-SEVEN

A new feeling came over Harvey as Melody was lifted onto the stretcher. He stumbled backwards over loose bricks on the ground, clutching at the wall, shrouded in disbelief.

"Harvey, are you there?" said Reg, his voice quiet in the haze of Harvey's mind. "Harvey, you need to get out of there."

But Harvey didn't reply. He couldn't reply. He was incapable of anything but watching Melody. Her body rocked from side to side as she was loaded into the ambulance.

"Harvey, I've got a fix on Dumas. Are you with me?"

It was Reg's voice, somewhere far away.

Something stirred inside Harvey as the ambulance doors slammed.

The light that spilt through the demolished doorway fell into shadow as a group of armed police approached. Their verbal commands were loud as they took control of the scene. Harvey slipped further into the shadows. Behind him was a set of wooden double doors, each with a small reinforced glass window at head height. Harvey peered through one.

"Where am I, Reg?" he asked.

"You're in the loading bay of Cannon Street Station," replied Reg. "To your left are the retail outlets, to your right, the offices. And directly in front of you is the main concourse."

"She's gone, Reg."

Reg paused before replying. It was clear he was fighting his own battle.

"Harvey, we need to focus. Do you want Dumas?"

Harvey didn't reply.

"He's in the station, Harvey. If we're going to get him, now's our chance. Are you with me?"

Harvey didn't reply.

"Harvey? Are you with me? Come on, I need you. Let's do this for Melody."

"For Melody," said Harvey.

He took a deep breath, rolled his neck and checked the small window in the door again. Crowds of confused and scared people were being ushered from the station.

"Harvey, I need you down at platform level in the underground. Can you get there?"

Outside, a heavy boot dislodged a loose brick on the floor. Harvey edged along, further down the corridor to his left out of sight.

"Guide me, Reg," he whispered.

"I've got you, Harvey. Keep going all the way to the end of the corridor and turn right."

Harvey followed Reg's instructions. The corridor was lit by emergency lighting, which cast an eerie green haze across the walls.

"We need to move fast, Harvey. I traced the signal that triggered the blast to a service tunnel one floor below you. There's been no signal since but they can't be far away."

Harvey peered through the doors. "Everyone's being evacuated, Reg. Do you think he'll mingle with the crowd?"

"No," Reg replied with confidence. "He's down there for a reason. That station will be cordoned off for the next few hours. The trains have all stopped, and the whole city is on lockdown. I'm sorry to say this, Harvey, but you're trapped in the city until further notice."

"No, Reg," said Harvey. "Dumas is trapped with me. Guide me to him."

"Okay, but your signal is getting weak. Any further underground and the GPS will give up."

"Where do I need to go?" asked Harvey.

"When you turn right, head through into the main concourse. The entrance to the underground is at the back of the building. Go down one set of escalators and there'll be a door right in front of you. That's where the signal came from. But after that, I don't know where they went."

"Got it," said Harvey. "See if you can take care of Melody. Find the hospital and get Smokey to call in a favour. Get her body out of there. I do not want her being pulled apart as evidence."

"Copy that, Harvey," said Reg, sounding strong, but his voice cracked, betraying his inner feelings.

The two doors thundered open with Harvey's kick. The noise was lost in the chaos of evacuating passengers but seemed to agitate the beast inside Harvey; it raised its head and cast a focused shroud over Harvey's vision.

The main concourse of the station was a one-way flow of tired and scared passengers, keen to get home, but forced back up onto the streets by police and emergency services. It was hard to blend in when everybody Harvey saw was walking in the opposite direction. A lone policeman was standing at the foot of the escalators directing people up onto the belt of stairs where many kept to one side, but most climbed up as fast as they could, eager to escape the confines of the station. A few people chose to walk up the stairs that ran beside the crammed escalators. Each of them gave Harvey a quizzical look as he strode past.

"Mate, we're being evacuated. You need to get out. There's a bomb," said one man.

But Harvey didn't reply. As he descended lower on the huge two-hundred-foot-long stairway, the doors to the service tunnel came into view exactly as Reg said they would.

The policeman did a double take when he saw Harvey coming down.

"No, mate, the station's closed. You'll need to go back up," he said. With one hand, he reached across Harvey and tried to steer him to join the masses of people boarding the escalator. With his other, he pointed back up the way Harvey had come.

Harvey continued forwards, pushing the officer's arm out of his way.

"Hey," said the policeman, suddenly turning his full attention to Harvey and gripping his leather jacket.

It took less than a second for Harvey to snap the man's arm back, twist his body around and pull the gun from his waistband. Harvey fired into the air three times and exactly as predicted, the slow-moving herd of people turned into a stampede.

Harvey shoved the policeman into the crowd, where he fell beneath trampling feet, and slipped through the double doors in the midst of the chaos.

CHAPTER TWENTY-EIGHT

A circular slab of concrete eighteen inches in diameter was pulled from the wall by thick, heavy eye bolts. Luca dropped it to the ground, rolled it out of the way and stepped back for Dumas to inspect the hole.

Dim light spilt through into the dark space from the room next door. Dante Dumas stepped aside and offered Lola a look with a sweep of his hand.

"And what will I see?" she asked, blinded by Luca's torchlight in her face.

"Freedom," he offered. "Or death. You choose."

Lola crouched, shone her own torch through the round hole and saw row after row of cages. Each cage looked to be ten feet square, with floor to ceiling reinforced mesh along each side and a thick steel gate at the front. The mesh obscured any view of the contents of each cage.

"What is it?" she asked.

"What do you want it to be?" replied Dumas, as if he was ready for the question.

"Okay, so what now?" said Lola. "I mean, I presume you have a plan?"

"Ladies first," said Dumas.

"Oh no," she replied, holding her hands up and standing away from the hole. "I'm not going in there. No chance."

Luca pulled a gun.

"So you chose death after all," said Dumas.

"Why don't you go in there? Or send one of your goons?" asked Lola. She flicked her head at Luca who stared back with cold, hard eyes.

"Oh, I'll be with you," said Dumas. "But it's a bit of a squeeze for these two."

"Why me?"

"Do you think we brought you for a picnic, or for your company? As nice as it is, no. You have a use."

"So it's a job and you need my expertise?"

"It's a vault, Lola. Your speciality," said Dumas, sounding slightly bored with the discussion and anxious to get inside. "So we do it my way, or not at all."

Luca's gun came back up and aimed at her head.

"We do it my way, Lola. Or not at all," repeated Dumas.

Lola took a look through the hole once more.

"Security?" she asked.

Dumas checked his watch, which sparkled in the torchlight.

"We have a forty minute window, so if you don't mind, Lola," said Dumas. "Marco, head back to the tunnel. Stop anyone who tries to get down here. Luca, get the transport."

Lola lay on her back in the hole and pulled herself through, dropping the few feet onto the dusty floor, then stood up and surveyed the cavernous room. The temptation to smash Dumas' head with the heavy Maglite as he came through was strong. But as pleasing as it would be, it would leave few options for escape with Luca on the other side of the wall and presumably guards, locks and cameras blocking the other exits.

For his age, Dumas was sprightly. He pulled himself through with ease, straightened and walked deeper into the room as if it were all one practised movement.

"Is it art?" asked Lola, as she washed her light across the locks of the cages and peered into one of them. Inside were rows of lockers, each marked with a five-digit number and a large keyhole top centre.

The next cage along was identical, and the next was similar but with larger lockers.

"It's here," called Dumas. He was in the next row of cages waiting patiently beside the lock. Lola joined him, glanced through the cage and saw exactly what she thought she would see.

"That's a Harris safe," she said.

Dumas held the bag out for her.

"Your tools," he said. "You have precisely twenty-five minutes."

"And if I fail?"

He raised his own gun and pointed it at her forehead.

"I believe in you. Failure is not an option, Lola."

"And the gate?" she asked. "Or do I have to open this as well?"

Dumas checked his watch, just as a metallic click announced that the magnetic lock had disengaged.

"Antonio?" she asked.

"He has his uses," replied Dumas. "No more talk. Open the damn safe."

Lola set to work, encouraged by sporadic reminders of the gun at the back of her head. Inside the bag was a calliper measuring tool, some chalk, a battery-powered magnetic drill, a diamond tip twelve-millimetre drill bit, a roll of electrical wire, and a fibre optic camera on a gooseneck, which connected to a tablet.

"It's all there," Dumas assured her. "Twenty-one minutes."

The centre of the lock was one hundred and twenty millimetres from the edge of the safe door, which was itself more than a metre wide by two metres tall. It was a safe designed for large objects and would weigh eight hundred kilos when empty.

Lola marked a vertical line with the chalk one hundred and twenty millimetres in from the door. Then she marked a small horizontal line one hundred and six millimetres above the centre of the locking spindle.

"What's that for?" asked Dumas. "You're not stalling for time, are you?"

"It's a Harris safe. It'll have a barrel inside one hundred millimetres in diameter. Surrounding that is a fifty-millimetre glass shield, which, if broken, will leak acid onto the porous moving parts. The heat of the chemical reaction will weld them together and render them useless. The safe would need to be burned open. We have a twelve-millimetre drill bit, so my hole will be precisely one hundred and six millimetres above the centre of the spindle. Then I'll mark one below for the camera, while I feed the electrical wire inside the top hole. If I can do that without breaking the glass, I can release the mechanism in a few seconds."

"You've worked with this safe before?" asked Dumas, impressed at Lola's knowledge and happy with his own choice of hires.

"Not this model, but it's a Harris. They went out of business a few years ago when Hamilton won the contracts for the major banks. There's still a few of these around, but not many."

"One less after tonight," said Dumas, as

Lola centred the magnetic drill and engaged the magnet.

"How long?" Lola asked.

Dumas checked his watch once more.

"Nineteen minutes," he replied, just as Lola hit the power button on the drill and drowned out his voice.

CHAPTER TWENTY-NINE

The doors hadn't yet closed on the stampede behind Harvey when a large fist came from nowhere and caught him in the face. He stumbled backwards, his weight forcing the doors shut, and barely managed to stay on his feet.

A large man in coveralls with tattoos on his neck and his hands was lining up for a follow-up attack. But he'd hit Harvey once. There wouldn't be a second time.

Harvey stood up straight, licked the blood from his lip and smiled as the man came at him with a wild untrained attack, which in Harvey's experience was based on sheer power and fear. He'd seen it too many times before; men had won fights by using the same approach and began believing that they could fight, thinking they were tougher than the rest of society.

It was also typical of these types of men to concentrate on head blows. While it was true that a well-delivered punch to the head could end a fight in seconds, the style of fighting had many flaws. Harvey thought back to his training with his mentor, Julios, and the words of wisdom that had kept Harvey alive for so many years. When you punch a man's head, you have more chances of breaking your own hand than his head. If the punch is not accurate, the man will not go down and you leave yourself open.

In true form, the man in the coveralls took a wild swing at Harvey's head, who simply leaned to one side and let the punch fly by, then delivered a lightning-fast jab to his gut. The man folded in two, shock widening his eyes. Harvey brought his knee up and connected with his opponent's nose. Then he held the sides of the man's head and followed up with his knee four more times, before slamming him down to the floor face first and pulling his arms behind his back.

Within a few moments, Harvey had removed the man's boot lace and hog-tied him with the lace running around the man's wrists and ankles with his legs bent up behind him. It was an efficient means of restraining a strong man that Harvey had used often in the past. The constant pressure from the legs trying to straighten tightened the knots and prevented movement in his hands. The man's sock was stuffed inside his mouth to stop him calling out if he came around.

The smooth tiled floor made sliding the man easy. Harvey pulled him around the first bend until he was out of sight of the entrance, in case some nosey policeman decided to peer through the doors.

Harvey rummaged through the man's pockets. A screwdriver, a pair of pliers, a Glock nineteen handgun, and a folding knife. It was useful. Wherever Dumas and the rest of his team were, it would be likely they would have Glocks too.

Harvey selected the pliers and pocketed the weapons as the man began to struggle against the restraints. He crouched down beside his face, which had turned bright red. His eyes flicked between anger and fear. Harvey watched him for a while in silence, until the man's anger had all but dissipated and fear flowed freely, bringing with it tears.

It had always intrigued Harvey how even the biggest and angriest of men cried. Many of them had cried from Harvey's presence, along with their own helplessness. Others required a few well thought-out questions to set them off, minimal words but carefully placed. Rarely did a man hold out so long that Harvey had to resort to violence. But when he did, the words flowed, free as a stream.

Being reduced to silent tears did not bring a man down in Harvey's estimation. It was natural, and he'd induced the emotions from so many men in the past that it no longer played any part in his judgement. Sobbing, the next phase of a man's breakdown, was irritating and border lined begging, which Harvey could not condone. Many men had begged for their lives between child-like sobs. At that point, Harvey always knew it was over for them. They were broken men.

Harvey opened the pliers.

It was confession time.

"I'm going to ask you a series of questions.

You are going to tell me the answers," said Harvey.

The man neither nodded in agreement nor demonstrated any hostility. He just looked up fearfully as Harvey ripped the sock from his mouth.

"What's your name?" asked Harvey.

The man did not reply.

Harvey hit him on the head with the pliers. It wasn't a hard blow, but it was enough to coax the man into talking.

"Who are you?" Harvey asked again.

"Marco," he replied, his face twisted in pain from the blow.

"Good. Marco, the more you talk, the less you suffer. Understood?"

After a few seconds' hesitation, more for a show of spirit than anything else, Marco nodded.

"Where is Dumas?" asked Harvey.

Only the sound of Marco's breathing came in reply. He dropped his face to the floor, fighting the urge to give up the information.

Without warning, Harvey grabbed a handful of his hair and shoved the nose of the pliers into Marco's mouth. He fixed on an incisor, then paused and watched as the realisation hit Marco. His eyes widened even further.

Harvey cracked the tooth back and forward, holding the struggling Marco still with his knee until the root finally gave in and the tooth came out. Harvey let it fall to the floor beside Marco's face, which was twisted with agony.

"Where's Dumas?" he asked once more.

Marco spat out a mouth full of blood.

"You've got thirty-one teeth left, Marco," said Harvey.

Marco shut his mouth and turned his head away, but Harvey's finger deep inside his eye socket was enough to force his mouth open and let out a scream. Harvey had to kneel on the side of his head to crack out the next tooth. A rear molar from Marco's lower jaw.

He dropped it beside the first. Tiny spatters of blood glowed red on the small white floor tiles.

Without waiting for answers, Harvey began to pull a third.

"Okay," said Marco. His tongue massaged his damaged gums as he spoke. He nodded with his head and gestured that Dumas had headed in that direction. "There. He's up there somewhere."

Harvey forced the pliers into his mouth once more. He latched onto a tooth and paused.

"Tell me where exactly," said Harvey. "Left or right. Show me with your hands."

With the pliers in his mouth and two bleeding gums, Marco could barely pronounce the words but waved his left hand, indicating that Dumas had taken the left tunnel.

Harvey wiped his hands on Marco's coveralls, straightened, and then bent to stuff the sock back into his mouth. He had just bent to wipe the pliers of his prints when movement caught his eye. In an instant, Harvey snatched his weapon from his waistband and stepped into a wide stance, aiming at the shadow in his peripheral vision.

The figure stopped still and raised his hands.

"How long have you been there?" asked Harvey, lowering his gun.

But the man, as small and slight as he was,

remained silent. Only an expression of awe was etched on his face.

"What are you doing here?" asked Harvey.

"I tracked her," said Fingers. "I'm here for Lola."

CHAPTER THIRTY

The diamond-tip drill bit took a while to break the steel surface, but once the outer skin had been chewed away, progress increased.

"How much longer?" asked Dumas.

Lola ignored him. One slip of concentration could break the drill bit and there was no spare in the bag. Dumas apparently took the hint. Lola felt him walk away, and from the corner of her eye, she saw him wander outside the cage to check on the main entrance to the vault.

Counting down the minutes in her head, Lola focused on the job at hand. Whilst maintaining consistent pressure on the handle with one hand, and squirting coolant onto the bit with the other, she ran through the motions of unlocking the safe once the holes had been drilled.

The electrical wire was thick. It would easily be sturdy enough to form a small loop in one end then feed it through the trigger. Once in place, another small length of wire would be used to pass through the loop and back out of the hole she had drilled. All that would be required then would be to pull on the two wires hard enough to raise the trigger, but not too hard that the loop would unwind. She would know when enough pressure had been applied as the spindle would spin without the clicks. She'd used the method before a few times but under less arduous circumstances.

Each manufacturer of a safe had a weakness that ran throughout their models. Harris safes were known to be almost unbreakable, save for the method that Lola was using.

A spindly burr of steel suddenly grew in length as the teeth of the drill bit reached the far side. Lola eased off the pressure to ensure the bit didn't shoot through the hole and break the glass vessel.

She powered off the drill and disengaged

the magnet. Then, holding the weight of the device with one hand, she manoeuvred the drill into place for the second hole.

"Fourteen minutes," called Dumas from the far side of the room. He'd heard the drill power down.

"That's five minutes for one hole," she replied. "Leaves me nine minutes to crack the lock once I've drilled the second hole."

"No, that leaves you four minutes to crack the lock," said Dumas. He stepped into view on the other side of the cage's mesh siding. Just his form was outlined in the low light. "We'll need five minutes to unload it."

"What's inside?" asked Lola, as she locked the magnet into place and collected the coolant in her spare hand.

"Dreams, Lola. I keep telling you."

Lola hit the power button again, bored with Dumas' vague responses. Drilling was fairly easy. Lola had learned when she was very young how to handle a drill. She had been taught by one of her father's friends, back in the days when Lola had been small enough to fit where most adults couldn't. The initial ten to twenty seconds were spent just warming up the steel and removing the outer skin to reveal the shiny, silver-coloured material below. Once the hole was outlined, and tiny strands of silvery steel curled from the drill, it was safe to increase the pressure a little. Keeping the bit cool was the trick. A broken drill bit cost time and added risk.

Dumas' shadow fell over her. He was back inside the cage.

"I need light," she said, without turning.

"You'll manage," he replied, without moving.

The battery in the drill began to wane as Lola reached two thirds of the thickness. The sound of the dying motor was lower in pitch. Lola remained quiet but glanced up at Dumas to see if he had noticed. He had. He smiled back at her and nodded slightly as if to convey his confidence in her ability to get the job done.

A long, curly burr of steel began to form at the base of the drill bit. The motor slowed some more. It was down to half speed. Lola eased off the pressure, removing all resistance from the drill. In a series of short bursts, she applied pressure for one second, then removed it. Another second, then removed it. The speed slowed to almost nothing with the familiar sound that accompanied a dying electric motor.

It stopped.

"Are you through?" asked Dumas.

Lola closed her eyes and let out a long breath.

"No," she replied. "Close, but no."

She didn't have to turn to know that Dumas had raised his gun and had it aimed at the back of her head. Thinking fast, she removed the battery pack from the drill, then wrapped it in her t-shirt. She rubbed as hard as she could for a few seconds to generate heat. The socket where the battery connected to the drill was dusty, so Lola blew on it and wiped the inside. Then she pulled the trigger without the battery to discharge the surplus energy.

She reconnected the battery, closed her eyes once more, and hit the power button. A surge of power turned the drill bit as Lola applied the pressure. Then she released it and shone her torch onto the hole.

"One more burst," she said to herself, willing the drill to turn. She hit the power button again and leaned into the handle.

The torque of the drill with her weight

tore through the remains of the steel sheet. Lola felt the give of the material in time to release the pressure and bring the drill back out. She switched the magnet off, dropped to the floor, and peered through the holes.

Dumas glanced at his watch, then peered past his wrist at Lola.

"You just bought yourself nine minutes of life."

CHAPTER THIRTY-ONE

"Where is she?" asked Fingers.

Harvey nodded behind him, further into the tunnel.

"It's Dumas?" asked Fingers.

Harvey didn't reply.

"So the robbery was a setup?" continued Fingers. "He wanted Lola all along?"

"Why would he want Lola?"

Fingers shrugged. "Maybe he needs her skills."

"Her skills?" asked Harvey.

"She's a thief, Harvey. The best there is."

"Why would Dumas need her? He's a thief too, right?"

"Maybe there's something he can't do,"

said Fingers. "She's excellent at diamonds and art, but she's really known for her ability to crack safes."

"Safes? Down here?" asked Harvey. "How did you find me anyway?"

"When Dumas took Lola, they hit me over the head. I've been stumbling around London looking for her." He held up his laptop satchel. "I managed to find an internet cafe and track her to the van."

Harvey didn't reply.

"I'm sorry, Harvey. I saw the explosion," said Fingers. "I saw them take your friend away. Melody."

The mention of Melody's name stabbed at Harvey's chest.

"I followed you into the building," continued Fingers. "I got caught up in the chaos outside, or I would have been here sooner."

But Harvey was deep in thought.

"Harvey?"

A familiar feeling began to push the grief to one side. It was a feeling Harvey had restrained for too long. A restless tingling began to creep into his fingers. His arms twitched as electricity seemed to course through his body.

Like a cage door had been opened inside

him, exposing his innermost feelings while releasing the beast that had stayed dormant for a long time, curious rage took a step into the wild once more.

The sensation of the beast within him roaming free triggered snapshots of his past. His first kill, deep inside Epping Forest. Back then, his rage was untamed, untrained and ferocious, enticed by the emotions of his dead sister, fuelled by the fear of his captive, and satiated by blood.

But the rage that now prowled Harvey's mind closed doors to reason. It quietened consequence with a slash of its sharp claws, and like a dog might guard its owner, the beast sought retribution for the pain in Harvey's heart.

"Harvey?" said Fingers. "Are you okay?"

But Harvey was enjoying the feeling of the beast now surging through his veins. Too long had he maintained control. A rhythmic pulse behind Harvey's dilated eyes kept time to the beating heart of the monster.

"Stop right there," came a voice, loud, clear and authoritative. It reverberated off the walls, obscuring any sense of distance.

But Harvey was trance-like. With his

palms open outward, his head tilted back and his eyes closed in a state of semi-meditation, anger and rage boiled inside him.

A hum of activity somewhere far off to Harvey's right. Fingers' voice. Panic.

The beast relinquished control of Harvey enough for him to assess the situation.

Fingers was on the floor, his hands cuffed behind his back just a few feet from Marco.

The police officer approached Harvey with a can of CS gas.

"Get down on the floor, or I'll be forced to-"

It took a fraction of a second for Harvey to break the man's arm, then another two seconds to slam him into the hard tiled wall. He let the officer fall to the floor beside Marco who lay with his face in a pool of congealing blood.

Harvey turned away and faced the empty tunnel in front of him, the beast by his side, angry and hungry for blood.

CHAPTER THIRTY-TWO

"I can't do this with a gun to my head, Dante," said Lola.

She had the first of the two lengths of wire threaded through the trigger mechanism. The tiny fibre optic camera had the loop in view and provided enough light.

The gun's hard barrel was removed from her head.

"No tricks, Lola," said Dumas.

She ignored the comment and continued to thread the second length of wire. The tiny LCD screen provided a magnified visual of what she was doing inside the safe door. The tiniest movement on the outside of the safe caused the end of the wire to shoot off the screen out of view.

She hooked the loop and slowly began to pull the excess wire back through the hole. The delicate work was complete. So she removed the camera and tossed it to one side. With two wires poking from a single hole in the safe door, she slowly increased the tension while feeling the spindle of the safe. When it spun without clicking, the lock would be free.

And there it was.

It didn't matter how many safes Lola had cracked before, the feeling was always the same. A sense of disbelief. Logic told her that the job was done, and all she had to do was turn the handle and the door would be unlocked. But a sense of dread loomed each time.

She reached for the handle.

"How long do I have?"

"Less than a minute," said Dumas.

She applied pressure to the handle, feeling the initial resistance of the locking mechanism search for the lock, but with the trigger free, the two plates that clamped down on the barrel spun with the handle.

The door opened.

Lola crouched down onto her heels and sucked in a lungful of air. The huge steel door swung past her face as Dumas opened it fully. The dim light of the room seemed to darken even deeper and the contents of the safe glowed a yellowish hue that framed Dumas in an almost godlike form.

"Gold?" she asked.

But Dumas was frozen in what seemed like a state of sheer adoration.

"This is my father's gold. It's beautiful, isn't it?" he said after a while.

Inside the safe, sitting in three rows of eight and piled four high, were ninety-six gold bars. Each one of them seemed to sing at Lola.

"Are we going to stand here looking at it?" asked Lola.

"Four minutes," said Dante, snapping to life. "One at a time, walk them to the hole." He reached down for the first one.

Lola watched him leave, carrying the bar in both hands, then stood up and gazed into the safe. Each bar bore a symbol of two crossed swords. She ran a finger over one, cursed at her situation, then picked it up.

She passed Dumas on her way to the hole and felt Luca's rough hands snatch the bar away from her. She bent to see where he was putting them, and to her surprise, beside the set of three steps was a train. Its doors were open and the carriage was empty.

As Lola and Dumas passed the bars through the hole, Luca and Antonio ferried them to the train, until Dumas emerged from the cage with the last bar, grinning from ear to ear.

But his delight was short lived. From behind him came a voice, loud and clear.

"Stop right there."

For a fraction of a second, Lola delighted in the look of failure that spread across Dumas' face. He turned to face the guard, who was standing poised with his radio.

"Put the bar down," the guard said. His taser was aimed at Dumas' chest.

Dumas took a step backwards in front of Lola.

"This is your last warning," said the guard. He glanced into the cage and saw the empty safe. "Where's the rest of the gold?"

Dumas remained silent. The atmosphere was electric. Lola was overcome with the urge to hit Dumas over the head with something.

Maybe the judges would go lightly on her. Maybe her father could help.

But sticking out from Dumas' waistband was his Glock.

She weighed up the odds of getting away with the heist. Given her record, she'd likely be an old lady by the time she'd be released from prison.

"Down," the guard shouted, and he re-aimed the taser.

Lola snatched the weapon from Dumas' belt and moved into an open space.

The guard froze.

"Drop it," said Lola.

"Good girl," said Dumas.

Slowly, the guard lowered the taser. His confidence was replaced by fear and the unknown.

"Drop the taser, sir," said Lola. "I don't want to have to do this."

The taser clattered to the floor.

"Kick it to me."

The guard did as he was told.

"Now get on your knees," said Lola, "and put your hands behind your head."

"I like your style, Lola," said Dumas.

But Lola switched her aim and pointed

the gun at him instead. "It's gone far enough, Dante."

"Lola, think about what you're doing."

"I can end all this right now," said Lola. "You lose."

"And what about you?" asked Dumas. "So you shoot me and then what? You can't walk out that door. The only way out for you is the hole. Marco and Luca might have something to say about that. I know Luca wouldn't mind seeing you suffer. He's been in prison for some time. I dread to think of the things he'd do to you."

Lola felt the gun waiver in her hand. The weight of the weapon, along with the shot of adrenaline that was releasing into her body, did little to help keep the gun held high.

Dumas took one step forward.

"I can make you rich, Lola, or I can make you dead."

Lola felt her face drop. Her hands locked. She was too frightened to move. The trigger was right there beneath her finger, but the command to move it was lost somewhere in the flow of adrenaline. A tiny bead of sweat ran down her forehead. It caught Dumas' eye.

He took another step.

"You did a good job, Lola, but it doesn't end here," said Dumas. "Now give me the weapon."

As he reached up and placed his hand around the barrel of the gun, Lola's brain issued the command to pull the trigger. But her body resisted. It was as if her survival instinct had taken over and understood that the only way out was through the hole, and the only chance of surviving that was with Dumas alive.

He tugged the weapon from her hands; they relinquished the gun easier than she thought. She let her arms drop to her sides. Dumas passed her the last gold bar.

"This one's for you."

At twelve kilos, the bar was heavier than the gun but felt weightless in the complex blend of emotions that fixed Lola in her stupor.

"Good girl," said Dumas once more.

Then he aimed the weapon at the guard, whose face contorted in a momentary expression of horror as Dumas pulled the trigger and ended the man's life.

CHAPTER THIRTY-THREE

Disabling the policeman barely touched the hunger of Harvey's beast. Instead, it aggravated his rage like an unreachable itch somewhere deep inside. Harvey's eyes streamed with adrenaline. His clammy hands hung by his side and the white, tiled walls of the tunnel slid past in an endless haze of memories, regret and pain.

He approached a fork in the tunnel. The left turn was smaller than the right but brighter and cleaner, perhaps because it was used more often. Harvey turned left, but as he did, his senses pricked. The hair on his nape was standing like men at arms and the beast inside him prepared itself.

With an almost imperceptible movement, Harvey slipped the gun from his jacket. He waited until he'd rounded enough of the bend to be out of sight for a second. One second was all he needed to turn and aim.

Footsteps approached, but not the steady drum-like rhythm of heavy boots, nor was the pace fast enough for it to be someone giving chase. Fingers walked into view then froze at having the gun pointed at him for the second time.

Neither man spoke, but Harvey lowered the gun and eyed him with caution. Fingers seemed to return the stare with his own weak blend of wonder and fear.

"How did you get free?" asked Harvey.

"The police officer," said Fingers. "I took his keys."

"And Marco?"

"Unconscious."

Harvey glanced back up the tunnel and listened for footsteps.

"I know you want to help her, but I can't protect you," said Harvey.

"I just want to get Lola somewhere safe," replied Fingers. His hands fumbled at nothing as if they should be doing something useful.

"Stay behind me. Stay quiet," said Harvey.

Fingers nodded.

Further underground, the air grew colder and the breeze brought with it the scent of dust and damp. There was no light at the end of the tunnel. No shining beacon of safety. And no Lola. Instead, in the distance, twenty metres from the final bend in the tunnel, a dark foreboding circle marked the end of the line.

"It's an underground tunnel," said Fingers. "Do you think the trains are running?"

Harvey didn't reply.

Two rats scurried along beneath the elevated rails a few feet below where Harvey was standing. To the right, the tunnel veered off around another bend. Only the whistling wind and its breath on Harvey's face indicated that the exit was further that way.

To his left, Harvey was surprised to see a train parked two hundred metres along the dark tunnel. A tiny concrete ledge ran along the side, presumably for workers to use to avoid the rails when they maintained the tracks.

A dull thud boomed from the train.

Harvey closed his eyes. There was a faint grumble of a man's voice.

He took a step closer. The voices came in waves as if the men were walking or moving.

Then a gunshot rang out. It was distant but definitely a gunshot.

Harvey's chest rose and fell as the beast inside him grew impatient. He let his eyes adjust to the poor light, rolled his neck from side to side, and took a step down onto the ledge.

Then, like a train hitting him from behind, the weight of a man slammed into Harvey. Thick arms wrapped around him and the momentum of the tackle sent both men over the ledge. Harvey landed with his stomach bent over a heavy rail. His gun clattered to the dark ground.

His attacker issued a growl from his place between the rails. The large shape of the man was swathed in the black of the tunnel. Only the sheer size of the man and the glistening of blood on his face betrayed his identity.

Without warning, Marco came at Harvey again, but his moves were slow. Harvey dodged the first blow and they squared off with the live rail between them, Harvey with his back to the service tunnel, Marco between the tracks. His bloodstained face, scarcely lit by the tunnel behind Harvey, accentuated the flaws in his skin. He grinned, bearing his missing teeth and spat blood to the ground, urging Harvey to come closer with two quick flicks of his hands.

"So you're the devil?" said Marco.

Harvey didn't reply.

Movement to his side, as Fingers began to walk along the ledge, caught his eye. But Harvey remained fixed on Marco. The beast needed feeding.

Marco stretched his leg out to the gun on the floor, but Harvey saw the move and stamped down on his foot. With the rail between them, the blows commenced.

A well-practised series of punches from Marco sent Harvey ducking, weaving and dodging, but the last, a right hook, caught his eye and knocked him off balance enough to step off Marco's foot. The bigger man was too slow to reach down for the gun before Harvey had recovered and returned with his own series of blows.

Fingers called out from further along the dark tunnel as Harvey rained blows to Marco's kidneys, ribs and stomach. As Marco turned to block Harvey's lightning-fast jabs to his left side, his right side opened up, allowing Harvey to deliver a powerful hook that broke at least one rib.

Inside Harvey, the restless beast began to settle into the fight. Each blow delivered was an appetiser for the main course. Each blow received was absorbed with guilty pleasure; it was punishment for his failure.

With both hands holding his ribcage, and his face contorted with pain, Marco straightened.

"Hit me," said Harvey.

But Marco made a poor attempt for the gun. With a smooth step across his side of the rail, Harvey kicked it deep into the darkness.

"Hit me," he shouted.

So Marco did. A straight jab to Harvey's face that bloodied his nose. But Marco retracted and adopted a defensive stance.

"More," screamed Harvey.

A hook slammed into his face. Harvey returned with a hook of his own.

"Again."

Once more, the blow caught him square and hard, and once more, he returned with a blow of his own. The rally of punches continued. Harvey roared with each delivery. Marco roared in defence. With each punch he received, Harvey's beast grew in strength, dispatching blows of his own, each harder than the punch before until both men wore a blood-red mask, their features obscured and swollen.

But from nowhere, maybe sensing Harvey's growing thirst for pain and strengthening retaliations, Marco broke the rally. He thrust out at Harvey and grabbed his throat with one hand, blocking Harvey's punches with the other. He dragged Harvey across the rail and slammed his forehead into Harvey's face. A wild, carnal roar emerged from Harvey's gut.

"More," he shouted and spat stringy blood at Marco.

Another head butt. Then, as the lights to Harvey's left grew brighter and the whining of the train's motors hummed loudly in the tunnel, the rails shuddered as if woken from their slumber.

Marco pinned Harvey to the single rail. The vibrations as one thousand tons of steel rolled towards them kicked at Harvey's back.

"You want to die?" Harvey screamed.

But Marco just grimaced from the effort it took to hold Harvey in place.

"Yeah?" continued Harvey. "Do you want it as much as me? Let's do it together."

Spittle flew from Marco's lip as the pressure on Harvey's neck increased. Harvey reached up and returned the move, pushing Marco away. The two men held each other's necks, but Harvey was pinned to the rail.

Harvey's eyes flicked to the train and back. Thirty metres and closing fast.

"You want to do this?" he shouted.

But before Marco could react, Harvey reversed the pressure. He pulled Marco towards him, knocking the bigger man off balance and turning him around so that Harvey was now pinning down Marco.

Twenty metres.

Harvey slammed his forehead into Marco's face.

Once.

Twice.

Three times.

Then, as the shadow of the underground train loomed above them, Harvey dropped to the floor.

The train rolled slowly overhead, sending

a whirlwind of dust and grit into the air all around him. Loud deafening booms of straining steel rails and wheels filled the tiny space. A shower of yellow sparks rained down on Harvey as electrical contacts brushed their steel counterparts.

The two halves of Marco's body slumped at Harvey's feet.

CHAPTER THIRTY-FOUR

Two big strong hands pulled Lola through the hole and slammed her up against the dirty wall. Luca's big head, silhouetted against the interior lights of the train behind him, leaned into Lola. The big man sniffed along her neck, savouring her scent, then issued a satisfied moan of delight as if he'd tasted a fine wine or a morsel of exquisite flavour in an excellent restaurant.

Behind him, Dumas scrambled through the hole. His coveralls stretched out onto the loose grit and dust, which showered to the floor when he stood up.

"No time for that, Luca," he said. "We've got a train to catch. Get ready to go."

Dumas stepped down behind them and onto the train, readying himself for the next part of his plan.

Luca lingered for a moment and although his face was shrouded in shadow, it wasn't hard for Lola to imagine his lustful leer.

"Get away from her," came a voice, familiar but weak. "Get away from her or I'll shoot you right now."

Luca took a single step back and turned sideways to reveal a man, slight, small, and holding a gun in two shaky hands.

"Fingers," said Lola. "No, run."

"And what are you going to do with that?" said Luca.

"He'll do nothing," said Dumas, stepping off the train with a gun to Fingers' head. "Nice try. Brave but stupid. Get on the damn train." Dumas waved his gun at the waiting train. "Both of you."

Fingers' face dropped from a tight but fearful expression of bravado to sudden panic and helplessness as it dawned on him the mistake he'd made.

Lola met his stare, but could only offer a sympathetic smile.

Both their lives were at risk, and Fingers had been her only chance of rescue.

"Let's go," called Dumas.

The tiny clicks of electrical switches sparked more lights into life as relays engaged, and capacitors hummed as energy built inside their wound copper bodies.

Lola stepped past Dumas and into the carriage. To her right, the door to the next carriage was open. At the far end was the driver's cab with Luca at the controls. To her left was a closed door and beyond that, the dark tunnel. Two large military cases on heavy casters were sitting by the doors.

"Into the first carriage," said Dumas. He followed them through, closing the door behind him.

"I'm connected," announced Antonio. When he saw Dumas enter, his voice changed, adopting a hint of apprehension. "I've cleared us a route out of the city, but we need to move fast. I don't know how long I can control the switches."

"Luca, go get Marco then get us out of here," said Dumas. "You two, sit." He gestured for Lola and Fingers to take two seats opposite each other.

The doors hissed closed and Lola's head rocked to one side as the initial burst of energy from the capacitors set the train in motion.

"Dante," called Luca from in front. "We have a problem."

"What is it?" called Dumas, then gestured for Lola to move ahead of him to the driver's cab. "Move."

"Dante?" said Luca again.

By the time Lola reached the door of the cab, Luca had slowed the train to a walk.

"What are you waiting for?" said Dumas, as he fought his way past Lola into the cab.

"It's Marco," said Luca. "He's on the tracks. But who's that he's fighting?"

A cruel smile spread cross Dumas' face.

"That's the devil," he said. "What are you waiting for? Run him down."

"But Marco-"

In an instant, Dumas had the gun raised and held it against Luca's temple.

"I said, run him down. He will move. He's not as stupid as he looks."

For a fraction of a second, a sense of hope quenched the butterflies that ran riot inside

Lola's stomach. The two men stared each other down in a silent battle of power.

Luca eased the train forwards. He cracked the window as far as it would open and called out for his brother to move and get on the train. But they were too far away and the deep grumble of the train as it rolled over the steel rails was too loud in the confines of the tunnel.

"I said forwards," said Dumas.

He slammed Luca's throttle hand forwards. Immediately, the train picked up speed, forcing Lola to reach for a handle that hung from the ceiling. She could see the battle ahead. Luca tried to pull the handle back and slow the train. But Marco and Harvey grew closer in the front windscreen. In the midst of their fight, Harvey had switched positions and had Marco pinned to the rail.

"No," cried Luca.

Time appeared to slow to a stop and the two men disappeared from view.

The bump of the wheels on the men's bodies was barely discernible as seventy tons of steel, glass and wood tore over them and ripped them to pieces.

Lola stood up, stunned.

Dumas released his grip on Luca's hand and rearmed his gun.

"You just doubled your pay. Now drive," he commanded, and stepped back into the carriage, pushing Lola with him. "Sit."

Lola sat down. She folded her arms across her stomach as her insides sought to spew anything and everything lose from her bowels and mouth.

A tear ran down Fingers' face opposite her.

Lola shook her head.

But Fingers lost control. He sniffed and sucked in a lungful of air and began to pant.

Dumas looked down at him.

"Don't worry. In fifteen minutes, it'll all be over," he said.

The statement did little to reassure Fingers, but his reaction served to amuse Dumas.

"Leave him alone," said Lola, having to raise her voice above the thundering train. "Can't you see he's scared?"

But Dumas ignored her, choosing instead to peer through the windscreen in the driver's cab.

Lola followed his eyes. Flashes of empty

stations rushed past. There was a burst of activity from one station as the authorities examined an empty carriage for more explosives. They reacted to Dumas' stolen train.

"I'm getting blocked out," called Antonio. "I think they're onto us."

"Can they shut the train down?" asked Dumas.

"No, I still have control of the power."

"Good. Keep control. It's not like they can put up a roadblock now, is it?" Dumas laughed.

He turned back to Lola, cast his eyes on the carriage behind with the gold, and then glanced at his watch.

However much Lola loathed Dumas, she couldn't help but admire his ability to retain his composure. The train hurtled past the authorities, police, the army and likely the special forces with more than half a ton of stolen gold on board, and at least four dead bodies in its wake. Dumas seemed to absorb it all as if he was untouchable.

But behind Dumas, through the windscreen at the front of the train, a bloodied hand rose up from below and slammed onto the glass.

CHAPTER THIRTY-FIVE

Fighting for purchase on the front of the train, Harvey held fast to the shunting ram with one hand and reached up with the other. He took hold of a small ridge in the train's steel body then stretched his leg out to the other ram.

With no weight to pull, the single carriage picked up speed quickly. The motion pinned Harvey to the train, and the tunnel sides flashed past in snapshot images of morphed pipes, cables and track. Then a bright station lit Harvey's world, revealing the next handhold.

The train accelerated. The wind that held him to the train was cold, stinging and full of grit, which stung his face and eyes, and the steel he clung to was hard and sharp.

With his left hand, he reached for the handhold, and with the other, he reached up and slammed his hand onto the glass.

No change in speed indicated that he'd been heard.

He pulled himself up.

Arranging his feet across both the shunting rams, Harvey straightened to full height and peered through the windscreen at the wide-eyed driver, who was dressed in coveralls, the same as Marco.

They passed another train. With just inches between the carriages, the force of the two huge, steel structures passing each other sucked Harvey to one side. But his feet were planted and his hands were strong.

The driver pushed forwards on the controls, accelerating the train even faster. Then, with a fresh blast of cold and a rush of wind that tried to suck Harvey from his position, the train broke free of the tunnel and into the night.

Exposed to the elements, he clung harder to his holds. Searching for a way into the train from the front, Harvey felt around for his next move and began to climb. But as he pulled himself up to the roof, shots tore through the reinforced glass. The last bullet of three ripped a chunk of rubber from his boot as he pulled himself out of view.

The train top was smooth with barely a crevice or crack to cling to, only a narrow channel on either side for the rain to drain off. A film of dirt and grime clung to the dried blood on his skin and the rushing wind pulled at every loose part of his clothing. Keeping as much of his body flat against the steel roof as possible, Harvey made his way along it inch by inch.

Several wild gunshots penetrated the roof, forcing Harvey to one side. He lost his grip on the right-hand gutter and slid down to the left, his fingers only just catching the narrow channel. It took all of his core strength to keep his legs from swinging down to the window and into view.

But from one side, five metres in front of him, he saw the passenger doors being forced open. The driver leaned out and peered up, looking for Harvey.

Harvey swung back onto the roof, opening his legs as far as he could, and watched helplessly as the man's arm swung onto the roof and fumbled for the rain gutter. With help from below, he pulled himself up to lay flat opposite Harvey.

At first, the man didn't move. Fear gripped him and his knuckles turned white with terror as he clung on for his life.

He began to slide closer to Harvey.

Sensing the oncoming danger, Harvey raised himself up to one foot, testing the train as a surfer might feel the movement of the board. Braving the wind that threatened to shear him from the roof, the man let go with one hand and reached behind him for his gun.

Harvey rose up onto both feet, bracing against the wind with his legs wide apart. He took a step forwards, coaxed further by the force of the moving train.

The man pulled his weapon and pushed up onto one knee. Holding fast with one hand, he raised the gun at Harvey.

Another step pushed Harvey forwards to within reach of the man, and as both men fought to balance, he reached out and grabbed the man's gun hand. With his foot, Harvey stamped down on the man's hand clinging to the train, sending them both reeling backwards along the train top. The gun fell between them. Both men eyed it, but only the bigger man made a move for it, which Harvey was counting on. The move opened up the man's defences.

Harvey began to get a feel for the moving train. He pinned the man's arm to the roof and, with his knee in the small of the man's back, Harvey delivered three blows to the back of his head. Each one slammed his face into the hard surface below.

But the man was wily and strong. He let go of the gun, spun beneath Harvey then rolled on top of him, pinning Harvey's shoulders down with his knees.

The gun slid along beside them, but neither man attempted to go for it.

With both fists, the man dealt a series of blows to Harvey's face, who was unable to move and unable to defend himself. Countless punches rocked Harvey's head until there was no longer any pain, just violent blows that snapped his head from side to side.

The loud horn of another train passing in the opposite direction shook them both and seemed to disrupt the flow of the man's punches. He threw one last hook, which

Harvey absorbed. He sucked in the power of the blow and with every piece of the animal fight inside him, Harvey fought to pull his arms free.

But the man on top of him was bigger and heavier. With a desperate kick of his right leg, Harvey hooked the man's neck and forced him backwards off his shoulders, then slid out from beneath him and rolled on top. As if a practised choreography, the man rolled with Harvey, reversing his move. He then stood up and backed away.

The reprise gave Harvey time to find his feet. Once more, the gun was between them. Once more, neither man made any attempt to reach it; both were content with the physical fight.

The train continued to roll over the rails. The surroundings had long since turned from the brick buildings of the city to the rows of apartments and old houses in the East End of London. The scene was slowly beginning to show more signs of green as the train cut through East London and into Essex.

It was as they passed through the town of Dagenham that, over the man's shoulder,

Harvey saw a bridge approaching; one mile away, maybe more.

With a roll of his neck, Harvey felt the satisfying clicks. He turned side on to Luca and adopted a judo stance he'd learned from his mentor, way back when the beast was born.

Luca moved with little grace into a street fighter's stance. It was the posture of a man who had learned how to fight by watching films, getting drunk in bars, and fighting men smaller than himself.

Luca dropped his arms and ran at Harvey.

Harvey held his ground, unmoving while facing the oncoming two-hundred-and-fifty-pound man until the very last moment, when Harvey dropped backwards, reached out, grabbed Luca's coveralls and raised his foot into the big man's stomach. The move was timed perfectly.

The bridge ripped Luca from Harvey's hands and left a fine mist of red spray in the air.

As the train rolled on under the night sky, Harvey lay back on the roof, allowing his heart to settle and his breath to return.

And the beast to savour its kill.

He searched for a way off the roof, deciding that the rear of the carriage would be safer to enter. But it was as he did so that a jolt rocked his balance, sending him to his knees. The train felt as if it was accelerating. Then Harvey realised that the rear carriage had broken free.

CHAPTER THIRTY-SIX

"You, inside. Drive the train," said Dumas. He pointed with his gun to the empty driver's cab.

"I can't drive the train," said Fingers. "I don't know how."

"Antonio, make sure she doesn't move," said Dumas. Then he pulled Fingers up by his hair and pushed him along the carriage into the cab. Dumas fumbled in Antonio's bag and pulled out a roll of duct tape, then disappeared into the cab.

"Why do you let him push you around like that?" asked Lola, keeping her voice low.

"I am a rich man," replied Antonio. He gestured at the second carriage with the two cases of gold.

A loud thud came from the roof, followed by a series of lighter thuds as the two men up top fought it out.

"Do you honestly think he's going to pay you? Do you honestly think that he has any loyalty to anyone but himself?" asked Lola. "Look at Marco. You saw what happened to him. And now Luca." She flicked her eyes up, but Antonio's remained fixed on hers. He was smart enough not to fall for the distraction.

He leaned in close to Lola, keeping the gun away from her reach.

"What makes you think I won't just take the gold myself?" said Antonio, his voice suddenly mature and confident.

He winked at her then moved away as Dumas emerged from the cab.

"Antonio, rig the last of the explosives to the accelerator," he said, without removing his eyes from Lola. Then he stepped closer to her. More loud thuds from above caused him to flick his eyes up. It was as if he was picturing the fight that was taking place on his behalf.

"You can't get away with this, Dante. They'll find you eventually. And if the police don't, my father will."

"Au contraire, my dear Lola. You see, we are

coming to the end of the line. Soon we will go our separate ways. I will seek a place in Spain so beautiful that even the most exquisite art, such as the Defeat of the Floating Batteries at Gibraltar, would not compare. And you? Well, there was a moment while you were cracking the safe that I thought you could be useful. I could get used to having a pretty woman like you around."

"Don't push your luck, Dumas."

"But alas, you have shown your true colours." He paused for a moment to let Lola digest his hideous, smug words. "They will find you and your friend in pieces, spread out as far as the eye can see." He spread his arms wide to accentuate the statement.

"And how do you plan on getting the gold to Spain? There'll be a manhunt out for that."

"Dear, when you have that amount of gold, you will be surprised, I think, at the levels to which people will go to please you. Blind eyes will be turned, palms will be crossed, and the sun will shine down on those bars as it did so many years ago. Its golden rays will kiss those golden bars, and the world will light up in glory."

Lola remained silent. No words could remove the madman from his dream. She'd seen that enough times with her own father.

"It is a day I have been waiting for all of my life, Lola. And I'd like to thank you for your help."

"You can thank me by letting us go."

"Sadly, no," he replied.

"The accelerator is rigged, Dante," said Antonio, as he stepped out of the cab. "We are getting close to the pickup."

"Good work, Antonio," replied Dumas. "Prepare to split the carriages."

He turned back to Lola, offering a weak expression of sorrow that conveyed more of his smug arrogance.

"Well, this is goodbye, Lola," he said. "I'll be sure to drop your father a line and tell him how brave you were." He finished by blowing her a kiss and moved towards the rear of the train. He opened the doors between the carriages, stepped across the small gap and winked at Lola once more.

"Antonio, let's move," he called.

Gathering his things, Antonio scrambled past Lola, hurrying to reach the second carriage before it was too late.

"You don't have to do this, Antonio," said Lola. "You're better than that."

Antonio stopped running and turned, but continued to walk backwards.

"You're a poor judge of character if you believe that, Lola."

He held her gaze for a moment, then turned and ran to the rear doors.

A jolt ran through the train as the carriages split just as they passed beneath a bridge. The few moments of the black outside made her feel as if she'd entered a new world. Above her, the roof rumbled as if something heavy was dragged at speed along the length of the train. A dark, twisted and ruined human form fell from the back of the carriage to the tracks below.

It was a world where the ticking clock of life ticked faster than ever before. And for a just a short time.

The second carriage was already far behind, slowed by friction, alone in a place where either side of the train tracks, open green, large lakes and clumps of trees spread far and wide as if they held the houses and office blocks at bay. It was a final stand for the environment in its war against urban sprawl.

"How are you doing in there, Fingers?" she called out.

A few seconds of silence passed before his timid voice returned, cracked and afraid.

"I need help," he replied. "I can't let go of the accelerator. I'm taped to it and they rigged it to blow if I move it. I'm bloody stuck, Lola. Help me."

"I'm cuffed to the seat, Fingers. I think we need to accept it."

"Do you know where we are?" asked Fingers.

"This is the District Line. There's about five more stations to pass through until we reach Upminster."

"What's at Upminster?"

"It's the end of the line, Fingers," called Lola. "It's the end of everything," she whispered to herself.

"No," screamed Fingers. "Not like this. This wasn't how it was meant to be."

Lola squeezed her eyes closed, restraining the tears that had begun to pool behind them.

"You've been a good friend, Fingers," she said, trying to convey strength in her voice. "The best I could have asked for."

The train hurtled through the town of

Hornchurch. The houses that backed onto the tracks blurred with tears and fog as memories swirled inside Lola's mind. With just minutes to live, she sought the memories she cherished most, for one last glance at them, to enjoy them one more time. But each time the memory of her mother and father swinging Lola by her arms as they walked through a long forgotten forest, or the memory of her mother's beaming face, bathed in sunlight as she handed Lola an ice-cream came to the front of her mind, the image of Harvey Stone torturing Cordero and her father's cold expression pushed them out the way.

It wasn't the memory Lola wanted to be thinking moments before she died. It wasn't how it was meant to be.

"Lola?" Fingers called out.

"I'm right here, Fingers. You and me together. Don't be afraid."

"That's just it, Lola," he replied. "I'm not afraid."

He stopped as if there was more to come. Lola pictured his face. He'd see the end before she would. It would be Fingers that saw the end coming. For her, it would be sudden, quick, and over before her brain registered the crash.

"I love you, Lola," he said. "I always have. Since we were young, all I ever wanted was to be close to you. To be the one you came to. To be the one who held you."

Words escaped Lola. His words hit her hard. They sucked the breath from her chest as if some unseen hand squeezed her heart tight.

"I'm sorry," Fingers continued. "I'm sorry I never told you. I'm sorry it had to be now. I'm sorry."

"No," said Lola, "don't be sorry. I'm here with you right now, and if there was anyone I'd want to be with in all this, it's you. I wish I could hold your hand, Fingers. I wish I could see your face."

"How long do we have?" Fingers called out.

"About three minutes would be my guess," Lola replied. She pulled at her handcuffs once more. But the effort was futile.

The rear door of the carriage banged hard against the train as it swung open. A river of tracks rushed past and disappeared into the darkness.

But there was a movement. A leg lowered into view. A black boot found a handrail. Then another.

Harvey Stone swung into the carriage and dropped to his knees. Then slowly, as if he was savouring the safety of the carriage, he raised his head and stared up at Lola.

CHAPTER THIRTY-SEVEN

"Reg, are you with me?" said Harvey as he stood up. He ran his forearm across his forehead, smearing Luca's blood across his face.

"Loud and clear, Harvey," replied Reg over the earpiece.

"Are you tracking me?" asked Harvey, as he strode through the carriage. He eyed Lola's cuffs and stepped into the driver's cab.

"I don't have a visual, but GPS tells me you're travelling at seventy miles an hour towards Upminster."

"Dumas is behind us somewhere. Get a visual on him. He's in a single carriage with two cases of gold somewhere near Dagenham.

My guess is that he's got some kind of escape planned by road."

"What about you?" asked Reg.

Harvey's eyes flicked from Fingers' frightened face to his bound hands and then followed the three thin wires that trailed from the driver's console down and into a small bag.

"Can you stop the train?"

"You're on a train?"

"Can you stop it, Reg? It's rigged to blow."

"How long do you have?"

"Look at the GPS."

"I'm looking now."

"Upminster is the end of the line."

"At seventy miles an hour you've got about two minutes, Harvey. It would take longer than that to hack the main system, let alone isolate a train."

"Can you do it, Reg?"

"No, Harvey. I'm sorry," said Reg.

It was the first time Harvey had ever heard Reg say that he couldn't do something. The news came like a breath of cold air.

"Find Dumas and stop him," said Harvey.

"What about you?" asked Reg.

Harvey searched for the words, seeking a plan, but nothing sprang to mind.

"I'll figure something out," said Harvey.

Reg seemed to hang on Harvey's words.

"Is that Reg?" asked Fingers.

Harvey nodded.

"Have him hack the Transport for London system. There's a chance he can access the switches to take us onto the British Rail line. It means we'll shoot through Upminster instead of slamming into the barriers. That should give us another thirty minutes as long as we don't hit something coming the other way."

"Reg, did you hear that?" asked Harvey.

"Already on it," said Reg. "Is that Fingers?"

"Yeah, he's tied to the accelerator. If he moves, it'll blow."

"Put him on the line," said Reg.

Harvey pulled the earpiece from his ear and placed it into Fingers', whose face was screwed up with thought, but he immediately began talking to Reg.

Harvey slipped from the cab and set to work on Lola's cuffs.

"We may have bought more time," he said, as he released her.

"How did you do that?" she asked, rubbing her wrist and flexing her arm.

"Someone taught me once," replied Harvey.

"A criminal?" asked Lola.

"No. A policewoman. Help me get the doors open in case we have to jump."

"Jump?" cried Lola. "I'm not-"

"Fair enough, but if Reg and Fingers can't work their magic, you'll be blown to kingdom come and I'll have a few broken bones. Your choice."

A few moments later, Lola was standing by Harvey's side as he worked his fingers between the sliding doors. A tiny slither of a gap grew to a finger space, enough for Lola's hands to reach in. She pulled on one door while Harvey pulled on the other until they were far enough apart for each of them to jump down onto the embankment below.

Finding the knife he'd taken from Marco, Harvey handed it to Lola.

"Cut Fingers free," he said.

"But what about the-"

"Just don't let him ease off the accelerator. Keep the pressure on."

Lola took the knife and moved away from Harvey, who was standing and looking out at the night, the rooftops of sleeping houses and the rushing trees. The air felt good and clean, cool and refreshing, but the cleanse failed to quieten the beast that grew restless inside his body.

"They did it," cried Lola from the driver's cab. She leaned through the single door. "Harvey, they did it. They changed the switches."

He glanced back at her, nodded and then returned his attention to more pressing matters.

The final station before Upminster flashed past in a blur of lights, then vanished, leaving only fluid memories of Melody in its wake. They played out like a reel of mismatched films, spliced with sadistic hands to form a looping nightmare of hellish design.

Like a lava bubble bursting, Harvey's eyes pulsed once. The throb of blood surged through him, seeking adrenaline, seeking...

Redemption.

A cool, familiar sweat formed on Harvey's nape. He found himself rolling his neck once more from side to side, delighting in the satisfying click with guilty pleasure.

"You die with me tonight," said Harvey to no-one but the beast.

CHAPTER THIRTY-EIGHT

"I'm sorry for what I said," said Fingers, as Lola pulled the tape from his hands and cut the excess off.

"Keep the pressure on," replied Lola. Then she let out a long breath. "It's okay. I knew. I always knew."

"You knew?" said Fingers. "And you let me-"

"You're my friend. You're a good friend. I don't want to lose that. I figured maybe one day, but-"

"But?" said Fingers, his voiced twinged with hope.

"But that day never came," said Lola.

"And it nearly never did," said Fingers. "What about now?"

Lola's eyes widened at the comment, but then she frowned and hushed her voice.

"You do realise we're standing beside a bomb, and I just had to cut your hands free? We nearly just died, Fingers, and you're asking me-"

"I'm asking if you feel any different now," said Fingers. "We bought ourselves more time, but we're still standing beside the bomb. So how about it?"

"You've put me on the spot a little, Fingers. Can I mull it over?"

"I'm not going anywhere," he said with a smile. "Can't we just wedge this accelerator open and jump? I feel so trapped."

"And send a seventy mile an hour bomb hurtling through the countryside?" said Lola. "Why don't you ask Reg if he knows anything about disarming a bag full of explosives?"

"Hey, Reg," said Fingers. "Are you there?"

There was a silence before Reg replied. Lola saw Fingers' face crease as he strived to hear Reg speak over the earpiece.

"Sorry you had to hear that," he said.

A blush of red filtered across Lola's face.

"Do you know how?" asked Fingers. His voice rose with excitement. Lola straightened. A glimmer of hope had shown its face.

Another silence.

"He needs photos," said Fingers. "Expose the wiring and use my phone, and don't miss anything out. He needs the full circuit."

Lola set to work pulling the bag away from the white bricks of explosives, being careful not to disrupt any of the cabling. She snapped five photos, found Reg's contact on Fingers' phone and sent them across.

"I didn't know you had his number on here," said Lola.

"He's one of the most talented technologists I've ever seen, Lola. It would be like you meeting Catwoman."

"Catwoman?" replied Lola. "Is that who you liken me to?"

Fingers seemed to ponder his answer with pursed lips and an amusing thoughtful upward gaze.

"Once or twice," he said, "but it was mainly about the outfit." He smiled a confident smile. But it flattened as his eyes fell back on his own hands, which held the accelerator lever away from the pair of wires.

"Hold on, he's back," said Fingers. Then he quietened as Reg relayed some instructions for Fingers to convey to Lola. "The circuit is using the train as the earth. There's a copper strap somewhere beneath the console that grounds the connections. We need to short the black wire against the copper strap, then cut the red wire. The explosives won't be disarmed but it'll mean we can ease off the throttle and wait for the bomb squad."

"Wait for the bomb squad?" said Lola. "You do realise I just helped rob a vault in the City of London, stole a bunch of gold, and aided and abetted a known criminal? Not to mention the murders that happened in between all that."

"Reg says we need to hurry because there's a train fifteen miles away and we're in its way," said Fingers.

Lola stared at the explosives, a small mass of wires sitting atop a few white bricks connected by a few random electrical components.

"We need some cable to create the short," said Fingers.

Lola turned the knife upside down and used the handle to smash through a few of the instruments on the driver's console. Once the glass was broken, she forced the dials through to reveal several bunches of cables below. One of them was as thick as a man's arm.

"Can I cut any of these?" she asked.

"How would I know?" said Fingers, peering into the hole.

Lola isolated a single, green cable. She pulled enough slack to give her a one-metre length, then closed her eyes, put the blade of the knife on the plastic coating, and sucked in a deep breath.

Then cut.

There was no explosion. No flash of light as the detonator sparked into life.

She pulled the cable out and twisted one end around the copper strap that grounded the console as Fingers relayed her actions to Reg for confirmation. She was standing poised with the other end of the cable in her hand and hovered above a small connector block on top of the brick of explosives, from which, the black cable ran to the accelerator.

"It needs to be a good solid connection, Lola. Twist it on as tight as you can," said Fingers.

She touched the wire in her hand to the black wire.

Nothing happened.

A few twists later and the circuit was complete.

"Now we can remove the black cable from the accelerator," said Fingers, repeating everything he heard Reg say as if he himself were the bomb disposal expert.

With barely a hint of hesitation, Lola ripped the black cable from the dashboard. Fingers pulled the accelerator back towards him.

The train began to slow.

Fingers pushed himself from the chair, and with unsolicited elation, Lola wrapped her arms around him. They hugged for longer than they cared. Fingers was the first to pull away, a little at first, but then he brought his hands up to Lola's face and held her, watching her as if it were for the first time.

Their kiss felt warm, natural and needed. Tension fell from Lola's muscles as water falls from rocks, as the two embraced and searched each other's bodies with elated hands, and the train rolled to a stop in the Essex countryside.

But the pleasure was short lived. A light

grew brighter in the driver's cab. A rumbling grew deeper and heavier.

Then the blast of an oncoming train sounding its horn fixed them to the spot in fright. Lola clung to Fingers, who held her tight and in the few seconds left, he stared in the face of the oncoming train, his whitening face a picture of resolve.

But when Lola opened her eyes again, the rumbling of the train, which had thundered past on the other tracks, began to fade away. Only the sound of a helicopter overhead remained. Its spotlight searched the ground around the train.

Fingers began to laugh, quietly at first, but then as Lola joined in, the laughter increased. They kissed once more in pleasure, thankfulness and gratitude.

Lola stepped from the driver's cab into the carriage.

"Harvey?" she called out.

"What's wrong?" asked Fingers, joining Lola at her side.

"He's gone."

CHAPTER THIRTY-NINE

For many years, Lola had shunned the wealth and power her father had accumulated, choosing to remain on the path her father had set her on when she had been a child. A thief of the highest order. But when the police officer had unlocked her cell door and ordered her outside, her father's wealth and power had come to fruition.

Shame embraced her as Samuel drove them through the magnificent iron gates of her father's estate. At the very worst, she thought, he would convey his outrage at her lack of trust in him, at her ability to break the family in two so easily, and then hug her as a father should. At the very best, he wouldn't acknowledge her insolence at all and start with a hug, choosing to save the discussion on trust for another day. Either way, she knew he would hug her, and she knew everything would be okay.

The grounds of her father's estate always carried within it a sense of peace and calm. The trees rocked with the gentle wind, but the movement was slight as if losing a leaf to the ground would disrupt the balance and order of the pristine landscaping.

The house itself bore a very different ambience. The hallway felt, and to Lola always had, as if it wallowed joyously in shadow. Dark wooden panels formed foreboding vertical lines that met with the intricate, looping designs of the mouldings, which ran across the walls. They formed frames of dark space filled with the heavy oil paintings that perhaps had once shone and glowed in the morning sun. But now they had succumbed to the bleak, hostile and unwelcoming entrance of the great house.

A few rooms in her father's house pleased her enough to raise her spirits. The greenhouse and pool room with their glazed roofs trapped the sun as a troll might trap a passerby, by reaching out from its cave and pulling inside its captive, leaving them with a view of the bright outside but surrounded by darkness.

The room Lola had called her own since as long as she could remember was south facing with a large balcony and floor-to-ceiling windows across two aspects. Thick curtains hung either side of the stone mullions but they were rarely closed. Her permanent reprise from the sombre house was adorned with bright, colourful pieces of art she had collected using her specialist skillset across close to two decades. Most of them were unknown paintings by unknown artists. But a favourite of hers that hung in front of her bed was a Dali, obscure, uncatalogued and full of intrigue without the need for shadows. The room was full of life, with fresh flowers each day, and walls as white as white could be. It was a stark contrast to the unsmiling perverse Caravaggios that stalked her journey to and from her room.

There was a gentle knock at her door.

"Come in, Samuel," she called out. She was standing at her balcony doors dressed in only a soft towel, looking out over the gardens to the world beyond.

"Ma'am," said Samuel, his usual precursor to a much more ornate and well-crafted sentence. He sucked in a lungful of air, but before he could speak, Lola interjected.

"My father wants to see me," she said. "You have prepared dinner, and he is seated."

Samuel gave a look of dejection at his own predictability.

"I'll be down in five minutes," she replied to his silence. "When I'm dressed."

She let her towel drop to the floor and padded to the six huge wardrobe doors.

"Is it a formal occasion?" she asked, as Samuel began to pull the door closed to leave.

He stopped, averting his eyes to the gardens.

"No, ma'am. Your father is in his robe. But we do have guests."

"Guests?"

"Three to be precise, ma'am."

"I see," said Lola, pulling her baggy pants from their hanger. "And father hasn't dressed for the occasion?"

"No. In fact, he's been in his robe since you were taken."

"Samuel?"

He turned to look at Lola, holding her eyes in his own in a conscious effort to prevent them from wandering where they shouldn't.

"Is he well?"

"I'm afraid he took a turn for the worse, ma'am. The whole episode has taken its toll on him. Mr Tenant has been a great help of course. But..."

"But?" said Lola. She pulled a fresh t-shirt from the shelf. "Oh, come on, Samuel, you've seen me naked a thousand times already."

"I'm afraid it never gets any easier, ma'am."

"And my father?"

"He needs his daughter. I'll confirm that you'll be down shortly."

Samuel left the room, but before the door closed fully, it reopened and he stepped back inside as Lola pulled her T-shirt down and flicked her hair out.

"Ma'am?" he said.

"Samuel?"

He seemed at ease now that she was dressed.

"I just wanted to say welcome home, ma'am." He bit his lower lip as if he thought he may have overstepped his mark. "I'm glad you're safe."

They shared a silent moment of appreciation for each other. Then Lola watched as Samuel closed the door fully, leaving her to finish dressing.

Her bare feet slapped on the parquet flooring a few moments later. The voyeuristic eyes of an eighteenth-century hooker sprawled across a chaise longue followed her to the staircase, where Angels Appearing to Shepherds and other Benjamin West pieces continued the accompaniment.

The conservatory was perhaps Lola's favourite room in the house. The light and airy feel with clean white surfaces appealed to her, along with the same view of the gardens that her balcony enjoyed.

Voices travelled along the long corridor like whispers of the paintings in the night. A deep grumble ceased all others. Her father's voice.

A light and self-conscious laugh, which was Fingers', was followed by a monotone, more confident inflection, Reg Tenant.

A silence fell, or so Lola thought. She stepped through the double doors to find all three men sitting around the large formal dining table that her father had relocated when he lost his leg. Each of the men was quiet, their attention captivated by the quiet words of a woman who was sitting beside Reg Tenant.

"Lola, come, dear. Join us," said her father. "We've been waiting for you."

Lola approached the table, hugged her father, and felt his gratitude through his strong arms. He wouldn't mention his emotions in front of guests. He didn't need to. Lola felt it.

She glanced around the room, nodded at Reg and grinned at Fingers. The woman eyed her with a curious friendly smile, flavoured with humility.

"I thought you were dead," said Lola.

CHAPTER FORTY

"It was close," said Melody. "I wasn't close enough for the blast to burn me, but the force threw me against the wall. The CCTV footage shows me bouncing off the brickwork. My head took the brunt of the impact and sent my body into shock."

"They released you so early?" said Lola. "It's been one week."

"No, your father had my recovery redirected here. I'm grounded until I get the all clear."

"I thought she'd stand a better chance of a full recovery here, rather than the four gloomy walls of a hospital," said Smokey.

"It's a very kind gesture," replied Melody.

"'The least I can do. My physician is one of the best in the country, and well, he visits me daily so it's really no bother at all."

Smokey picked up his wine glass.

"I'd like to raise a toast," he began. "We set out to save the Defeat of the Floating Batteries at Gibraltar, and we did so with gusto. Along the way though, I learned a most valuable lesson. Lola dear..." He reached out and held her hand on the table. "Please forgive me. I lost sight of what is truly important, and for that, I can only apologise."

"You don't need to-"

"But I am, and I will," Smokey interrupted. "It is the job of the living to preserve the art on the walls of this house and in the homes and galleries around the world, so that generations to come may enjoy them as we have. But not at the cost of lives. How can we enjoy, admire or question art when the very essence of ourselves lies in fragments? Dumas may still be out there with the gold, but I feel it will be a long time before he returns to darken our days."

"Father, you're forgiven," said Lola. "Let's eat."

With a tear in his eye, Smokey raised his glass.

"What are we toasting?" asked Reg.

All eyes fell on Smokey as he sought a suitable choice of words. Melody tried to guess what he'd say during the tiny moment of silence. Perhaps a few words for Harvey or for the risk everybody took. But once more, Smokey surprised her.

"Life," he said.

"To life," everybody repeated.

But Fingers still held his glass high as others sipped at their wine, and Melody placed her water on the table.

"And love," said Fingers. His eyes locked with Lola's and the two shared a moment.

"Are you okay, Melody? Are you comfortable?" said Lola.

"There's still one of us missing," she replied.

The room hushed.

"I'm sorry, Smokey. I can't enjoy this meal knowing that he's still out there risking his life while we toast to life and love. If it wasn't for him, some of us wouldn't be here at all today."

"And how do you suggest we make amends?" asked Smokey.

Melody turned to Reg.

"Can we track him?" she asked.

But Reg shook his head.

"He has no phone and no tracker. He's untraceable."

"But there must be something we can do," said Lola. "I feel simply awful." She returned her cutlery to the table.

"Where will he go?" asked Smokey. "I understand he has a house in France?"

"No, he won't go there. He won't stop until he finishes the job."

"Do you think he'll carry on after the gold?" asked Fingers. "Dumas will be long gone by now."

"No, Harvey won't care about the gold. He thinks I'm dead. He'll be on Dumas' heels and won't stop until..."

She stopped before the sentence became inappropriate for the dinner table.

"Until what, Melody?" asked Smokey.

It was Melody's turn to feel the burn of everybody's eyes as she sought the right words. She looked up at Reg, the one person in the room who understood Harvey as Melody did.

"Until he's broken Dumas," said Reg.

"Until he's found him, hung him up and torn every piece of his flesh from his still-breathing body. Even then he won't stop."

Reg held Melody's gaze and spoke the words as if they were his own. As if he himself was capable of the things of which he spoke. The punishment.

"Retribution?" asked Smokey.

"We need to find Dumas," said Lola. "If we can track Dumas, we'll find Harvey."

"Yeah, but how do we find Dumas?" asked Fingers. "If we could find Dumas, then surely we could get the gold back."

"We lure him out," said Smokey.

"And how do you suppose we do that?" asked Fingers. He folded his arms across his chest and leaned on the dining table.

"What's the one thing Dumas wants but can't have?"

Melody saw it coming. But by the looks on the faces of the others, nobody else had fallen in yet.

"Me," said Smokey. "He wants me dead."

"No, father," cried Lola.

"Samuel?" Smokey interrupted with a hand raised to quieten his daughter.

Samuel stepped forwards, his raised eyebrows inviting his employer's order.

"Prepare the jet. We're going to Spain."

CHAPTER FORTY-ONE

"You have to understand, Lola," said Smokey. "How can I go on not knowing if Harvey is alive or dead? If he is dead, then it's my fault and I should pay the price."

"There has to be another way," said Lola.

The light above her seat pinged on, illuminating the outline of a seat belt.

"If Harvey is alive, we can stop him. He doesn't know Melody is alive. Perhaps if he knew, he would stop."

"And you would stop too? We can call the whole thing off?" asked Lola.

Smokey's private Learjet jolted into life. The tarmac began to roll past the window as the pilot positioned the plane at the end of the runway.

"Maybe," said Smokey. "The truth is, Lola, that I do not know what will happen until we draw Dumas from his hiding place."

"And how do you know he'll be in Punta Secreta?"

"Do you remember the painting, the Defeat of the Floating Batteries at Gibraltar?"

"How could I ever forget?"

"Punta Secreta is directly opposite Gibraltar on the Spanish coast. It is a small town, overshadowed by Algericas, but its history is strong."

"And that's what makes you think Dumas will be there?"

"No, my dear. Dante Dumas' family used to rule the area, many years ago, before even my grandfather's grandfather was born. It was a time when the Spanish were a force to be reckoned with. But when the British spread their wings, the Spanish were pushed to one side. The war that had been fought for so many years at sea finally came to the land. Entire towns were wiped out. Families were erased from history as if they never existed."

"The Defeat of the Floating Batteries at Gibraltar," said Lola.

"A tiny moment in such a tragic time, but poignant nonetheless," replied her father. "If Dumas is settling down in Spain with his new-found wealth, that's where he'll be."

"So how do we find him?" asked Lola.

"We don't. He'll find us."

"You are going to walk into the lion's den? He will have men there."

"Yes, I imagine he will have loyalty. His family's name lies at the very root of the town."

"And how do you expect to stop him?"

"I don't Lola," said her father. "If Harvey is there, he will stop Dumas."

"And if Harvey isn't there?" said Lola. "Have you even considered that?"

"Then, my dear, you have to prepare yourself for the worst."

"No, Dad. No. You can't do this. I won't let you."

"Lola, Lola, please."

He rested his hand on hers and squeezed it tight. But his hands were fragile. The squeeze was nothing compared to what it used to be. She hadn't seen before, but now it was clear. Her father's frailty had crept in like a weed might infiltrate a flower bed, growing and taking root under the cover of darkness, deep within the soil. And then one day, when it is all but too late for the plant, the weed reveals its finest work.

"If we cannot stop Dumas, then he must stop me, Lola. It is the only way that you will live a quiet life without me."

A single tear fell from Lola's eye. It dripped onto her face and ran along her cheek, unhindered by flaws to her lip, where it hung and fell.

"I've made all the arrangements, Lola. The estate-"

"Stop," she said. "Just stop. Harvey will be there. I'm not coming back without you."

"I don't expect you to come back without me, Lola." He reached across, held her hand in his and gave it a soft squeeze. Then he smiled his trademark childish smile. "I just might be in a box is all."

CHAPTER FORTY-TWO

"Okay, listen up everyone," said Melody, as the plane taxied off the runway at a small airstrip outside Punta Carnero.

Melody was standing at the bulkhead addressing Smokey, Lola, Samuel, Reg and Fingers as if she was briefing a team of black ops specialists about to go behind enemy lines.

"We have one objective, and that is to bring back Harvey. The current status is that he thinks I'm dead, and due to his nature, he'll be seeking revenge. We're all aware of the type of revenge that Harvey is capable of. If we can avoid that and get out before Dumas knows we're even here, we'll be fine. But if

Dumas gets wind of us, things could go south very fast. This is his hometown. He has allies here. We do not."

The team looked back at her with nothing short of admiration. Her confidence and the general manner in which she carried herself gave weight to the speech she was making. Not a soul disrupted her.

"We know that Harvey is after Dumas. We also know that Dumas and Smokey are old enemies." She paused before continuing. The statement needed to be made but she selected her words as a surgeon might select a scalpel. "We know that Dumas would go to lengths to have Smokey killed. We're going to avoid that at all costs."

She held Smokey's appreciative stare and ignored Lola's tearful expression in her peripheral.

"Smokey and Lola will venture through the town as tourists. There are a few hotels, restaurants and beaches. Tourists aren't out of place. I will be shadowing them. The moment Dumas makes an appearance, we need to be on the ball. If Harvey is here, you can bet your life that he'll be close by."

"And us?" asked Reg. He was sitting beside Fingers. Both men had their laptops out in front of them and had spent the flight comparing codes for software that they had designed.

"Samuel has made the arrangements for a hotel. You'll be comfortable. It has internet and coffee. Do you need anything else?"

Both Fingers and Reg shook their heads.

"We will all be wearing GPS trackers. We will all stay in communication. And we will all be leaving here in one piece."

"How do you plan on getting Harvey to come with us?" asked Lola.

"Leave Harvey Stone to me, Lola. He thinks I'm dead. He'll slaughter anyone he thinks played a part in that. When he sees I'm alive, he'll stop."

"And you get to fly off into the sunset with your man?" said Lola.

"And we get to stop any more bloodshed, Lola," replied Melody. "Enough people have died."

"And the gold?" asked Smokey.

The statement was out of place. Melody mulled it over before replying.

"The gold is not our concern, Smokey."

"But if we can save it?"

"The gold is not our concern, Smokey." She let her answer hang for a moment. "Is everyone clear on what we're doing?"

Everyone nodded and began to stand from their seats.

"Samuel," said Melody, "how about being the designated driver?"

"Thought you'd never ask," Samuel replied.

At the foot of the steps, two officials checked their passports for the EU symbol, confirmed the photo was an accurate reflection of the passport holder, and then guided them to a waiting mini-van.

Melody slammed the side door, then moved to the passenger seat. She leaned inside.

"Mind if I ride shotgun?" she asked.

"Not at all," replied Samuel. "Do you know where you're going?"

"It's a small town. I did some research on the flight. We'll drop the boys off at the hotel, then head into town. Drop me off somewhere out of sight and take Smokey and Lola to a restaurant."

"Copy that," said Samuel. For the first

time, his voice lost its submissive edge.

"Were you always a butler, Samuel?"

"Not always."

He pulled away from the airport onto a narrow lane. In the distance, irregular rows of white-washed houses, dotted with pastel blues and hues of yellow, built within small plots of land across the hillside. The sea lay beyond the town, blue and sparkling. Samuel settled into the drive, maintaining the forty kilometres per hour speed limit.

On the left, atop a green hill, was a castle.

"Two hundred years old," said Samuel, catching Melody's gaze. "Built to stop the English encroaching any further."

"You've been here before?" asked Melody.

"It's a small town. I did some research on the flight," replied Samuel.

Melody fought to restrain her grin.

"Have you worked for Smokey for long?" she asked.

"Long enough to know better, and too long to change things now," he replied. "Besides, who'd look after them if I left?"

"So you're part of the family? That's nice."

"I'm their butler. They pay me to serve them."

"But surely, over the years-"

"Over the years, Melody, I've seen Lola grow up. I've seen my employer lose his wife. And I've seen more than any man should have to keep quiet about in ten lifetimes."

"So it's a mutual understanding then?"

"They need me, and I need them."

"No," said Melody. "You're family. You just don't like to admit it."

The gentle ribbing brought a smile to Melody's face. She wondered when was the last time she smiled.

"He's special to you, isn't he?" asked Samuel.

Melody didn't reply.

"Come on. I showed you mine," said Samuel. "Give a little."

Melody nodded softly. The smile faded.

"He's nothing to me. He's everything to me. He's a part of me."

Samuel let out a soft whistle of air between pursed lips.

"Deep," he said.

"You asked."

"And you can control him?" asked Samuel. "I mean, you really think you can bring him in and stop him?"

"You know what, Samuel? I'm the only one on this planet that stands a chance."

She looked back out of the window.

"If I fail, I wouldn't be surprised if he slaughtered the whole town trying to find Dumas."

CHAPTER FORTY-THREE

"Comms check everyone," said Melody. "Let me know you're online."

"Copy," said Reg and Fingers.

Melody turned to face the rear of the van and slid the glass window open.

"I hear you," said Smokey.

"Copy," said Lola.

"Samuel?" asked Melody.

"I hear you," he replied.

"Okay, good. We're all here. Remember to keep the channel open. Tell us everything that's going on no matter how trivial. Reg, Fingers, do you have the satellite link yet?"

"Yes, we've borrowed access to an international satellite," said Reg.

"Good. Keep your eyes and ears open." She turned around to face the rear of the van again. "Okay, let's do this."

The sliding side door of the mini-van slid open, and Samuel reached in to set the ramps for the wheelchair. Between them, Samuel and Lola eased Smokey from the van.

"Pass me my crutches, Samuel."

"But, Father-"

"Just pass me the crutches. I'm not being stuck in this damn thing all day. It's hotter than the sun here and there are more potholes than road."

Samuel held the crutches steady while Lola helped her father from the chair. Then she collapsed the chair and slid it back into the van.

"There," said her father, "I'm just as tall as the rest of you for once. How about lunch, Lola?"

Samuel climbed back into the van as Lola leaned into the side door to talk to Melody.

"We'll be here an hour or so, maybe a little more. Then we'll move on to somewhere else."

"Okay. I'll have Samuel drop me some-where close by. You won't see me, but I'll be with you every step of the way."

She slammed the door, then put her hand on her father's arm to help him cross the road. Behind them, a few houses were sitting like stepping stones before the Mediterranean. In front of them, the Blue Lagoon restaurant was perched on a small, rocky knoll.

"How wonderfully Mediterranean," said her father, as Lola urged him across the road between the sparse traffic. A set of steep stairs led to the restaurant from the roadside, but to the side of the building, a ramp for cars to access the car park proved to be more suitable for Smokey's crutches.

The effort took ten minutes, but soon, they were both being seated on the veranda with an open view of the sea. Terracotta rooftops and bougainvillaea struck colour to the whitewashed foreground while grassy patches adorned the limestone ground below.

"So beautiful," said her father. "It's only when you come to a place like this that you wonder what on earth you've been doing with your life."

The statement required no answer. Lola allowed her father to muse. The fresh sea air would do him good.

She caught the attention of a waiter and

ordered a sparkling water and a salad. Her father ordered the fish with a crisp white wine, then leaned back and sucked in the air.

"We needed this, Lola," he said. "After what we've been through these past few weeks, we really did need this. Yes, we did."

"You're not forgetting why we're here, are you?" she asked. "It's not a holiday."

"Oh, but it should be," he replied, his voice full of dejection. "It weighs heavy on my heart, my dear. We force ourselves into stressful lives allowing for a few weeks a year to come and relax in a place like this. We've got it all wrong, haven't we?"

"I imagine that a life here would come with its own challenges, Father. It's not ex-actly booming, is it?"

"Given the choice, Lola, would you have the financial assurance we enjoy and the asso-ciated luxuries, or would you trade it all for a life somewhere like this, not knowing if you'll have money for food next month?"

"Is that a loaded question, Father?" She smiled. "Are you trying to tell me something?"

"No, of course not. But you've never had to go without. You haven't experienced it, and that's what I always wanted, for my family to be looked after."

The waiter slipped between them with his tray. He cracked the sparkling water bottle open and poured a glass for Lola over ice and lemon, then poured a little wine for Smokey. Smokey collected the glass between his finger and thumb then swirled the wine. The thin layer of residue emitted a scent that Smokey inhaled. He took a small sip of the wine, let the flavours separate in his mouth and then placed the glass on the table with a nod to the waiter, who poured half a glass for him.

"Please," said Smokey, "leave the bottle."

"As you wish, sir," the waiter replied in his thick Spanish accent. "I will bring your food in a little while, but please, I will be here if you would like something else."

"Thank you," said Smokey, as the waiter left them alone.

"Samuel could get some tips from him," said Smokey.

"Do you think Dumas will show?" asked Lola. "I mean, do you think our arrival has been noticed?"

"Something tells me yes," her father replied. "He will have his spies out for sure. I imagine that the villagers would be more than willing to feed him information for a slice of his pie."

A short while later, when Smokey had folded his serviette and placed it over his half-finished fish and Lola had finished her salad, the two relaxed back in peace and stared up at the castle that was sitting atop the hill over-looking the Mediterranean and Gibraltar.

"It's hard to think that two hundred years ago this place was ravaged by the atrocities of war, isn't it?" said Lola's father.

"I can't see them moving any faster than they do now," replied Lola. "There's hardly a lunchtime rush, is there?"

"Shall we get the bill and venture else-where?" suggested Smokey.

Lola flagged down the waiter, who approached with a smile from loitering on the next table, which Lola had guessed was just a display to be on hand when the rich tourists wanted something, a ploy to increase the generosity of the tip.

"Could we get the bill, por favor?" she asked.

"The bill?" he replied. "No, your meal is on the house. I do hope you enjoyed it?"

"It was fantastic, thank you. But why is it on the house?"

"Please," replied the waiter, and with an open hand, he guided their eyes to the man who was sitting in the corner beneath a cream hat in a black shirt and white pants.

"Señor Dumas will see you now."

CHAPTER FORTY-FOUR

Opposite the Blue Lagoon restaurant in a derelict house, Melody was standing in the shadows with a one-hundred-and-eighty-degree view of the street and the rooftops above. The doors of the house had long since fallen off or been removed to service another house nearby. The windows were mostly intact, but the collapsed ceiling offered ample accommodation for local birds to nest.

A few cars passed by, and while Reg and Fingers ran the plates, Melody scanned the drivers, judging them to be safe, potential or a direct threat based on appearances. The three drivers, two of which were elderly and one of which was a local man in his pickup with a goat in the back, had all been marked as safe. Their number plates supported their innocence.

"Looks like they're finishing up eating," said Melody. "They'll be moving soon. Can you guys run a check on the street? Make sure there's no parked cars, vans or loitering people. Identify the potential threats, Reg."

"We're on it," came Reg's reply. "We have a blue Nissan two hundred yards to your right, and a silver Mercedes to your left, and half a dozen motorcycles within a five hundred yard radius of the restaurant. The only thing we've seen move is the three cars that passed and Samuel's van, which is parked two hundred yards away on the coast. Everything else has been foot traffic."

"Only three cars moved in the thirty minutes we've been here?" said Melody. "Is this place asleep, or what?"

"The entire village would fit on a few football pitches. I guess they don't need cars to get around."

"Well, it should make spotting Dumas easier," said Melody. "Sit tight. Smokey and Lola are moving. Do you have eyes on them?"

"We do. It looks like they're talking to someone," said Fingers.

"Can you get a look at his face?"

"Negative," said Fingers. "He's wearing a hat."

"Okay, I've got him," replied Melody. "White hat, black shirt, and white pants?"

"That's him," said Fingers. "They're sitting down with him. Do you think it's Dumas?"

"You tell me, Fingers. You're the only one here who's seen him."

"I can't see a thing with that hat."

"Okay," said Melody. "Scan the area and watch for Harvey. He may be close. I'll see if I can find a different angle and send you a photo. Do you guys have facial recognition?"

"Yes," said Reg. "I have access to LUCY."

"Give me two minutes," said Melody, and she slipped back into the shadows.

"They're moving, Melody. Do you have a visual?"

"No, I'm at the back of the house. Talk me through it."

"Smokey's on crutches in front. Lola and the guy in white are walking behind. They're heading to the car park."

"Any sign of Harvey?" she asked.

"Negative, Melody. It's dead down there."

"I need to get a visual on this guy. If it is Dumas, Harvey won't be far away."

In true Mediterranean style, the ground floor of the tiny house was divided into a reception room and a south-facing kitchen with a back door to a rocky and barren yard. A few old chairs were scattered around the plot as if someday, a long time ago, the view across the Med was enjoyed with a sangria or two.

The neighbouring house, in all its glory with the terracotta roof, bougainvillea-lined yard and immaculate lawn furniture beamed with life, in stark contrast to where Melody was standing. She eyed the property for movement. There were no open windows, despite the heat of the day. There was no car parked outside in the rocky driveway.

"Reg, am I clear to move? The house next door looks empty. Tell me what you see."

"I see no movement. No heat signal. And the roads are clear. Go."

She glanced around one last time then shoved off the wall to make a run for it. But a hand swept across her face from behind. She sucked in a lungful of thick chemical fumes. She knew the smell, but the fog overcame her regardless. Darkness crept into her vision from all sides, leaving a diminishing circle of light.

Then black.

"Nice of you to pop by my little town," said Dumas. "How do you like it so far?"

He was sitting with his legs crossed and his hat pulled down across the top half of his face. A slither of eyes stared out at Lola and Smokey.

"We've only seen this place so far," said Lola. "But it's not bad. The salad was limp, but I can't complain."

"I watched you arrive. That's a nice van you have there, Smokey. Times are good for you right now, I see."

"I could say the same for your yacht," replied Smokey. "I can only assume it's yours.

There doesn't seem to be any other money in this hole."

"Beautiful, isn't she?" replied Dumas. "It gets me around at a pace I enjoy."

"I'm sure it does, Dante," said Smokey.

"I'd like to show you something. Would you join me?"

"And if we said no?"

Dumas raised an eyebrow. His eyes flicked across at two men who were sitting at a nearby table. They were both dressed casually with dark hair, weathered skin and lean muscular arms from a life on the sea.

"It's amazing how the spirits of the local people are uplifted when prosperity docks in their bay," said Dumas.

Lola glanced out to sea at the yacht that was moored inside the breakwater.

"Prosperity?" she asked.

"I named her myself," replied Dumas. "Fitting, isn't it?"

"That depends on your definition of prosperity, Dante," said Lola.

"Before we leave," said Dumas, ignoring Lola's comment, "you haven't told me what you're doing here."

"It's a nice place. The sun is shining."

"What a coincidence that you should run into me then, Smokey. Of all the coastal paradises in all the world."

"How long before you ruin it, Dante?"

"You've come for me, haven't you? Well before you get carried away, you should know that beneath the sleepy façade, this town is my home. These are my people. All I have to do is say the word and poof." Dumas animated his threat with jazz hands, then let them fall to his lap. "We've known each other a very long time, Smokey. Did you know, Lola, your father and I used to be in competition? I'm sure he's told you the stories. You see, we both had similar backgrounds. Our families both lost their wealth but your father and I managed to find it again. Aside from the obvious physical differences, we are but the same man inside."

"You couldn't be more wrong, Dumas," said Lola.

"Tell me about Cordero. Was it fun to watch him suffer?" asked Dumas. His eyes flicked to Lola's chest then returned, unashamed. "Where we will go was once my family home. For the time being, I am but a caretaker, but soon it will be in my family once more, and everything that was shall be again. I think it's rather poetic. Don't you, Lola dear?"

Lola bit her tongue.

"You keep looking around, Lola. Are you expecting company?" Dumas' head cocked to one side, ready to contemplate her next words. But Lola remained silent.

"Well, folks, if that is all we have to say, I suggest we take a short drive."

"And where is it we're going?"

Dumas rose from his chair, leaned over the table and seemed to inspect Lola's hair.

"Remove it," he said.

"Remove what?" Lola protested.

"The earpieces. Remove them. Both of you." His voice had grown abrupt and his eyes narrowed as both Lola and Smokey removed the earpieces and placed them on the table.

"If I ask you how many, you will only insult me with lies. So I will leave it there. But know this, there is no escape for you both, and if anybody tries to stop me now, they will be fish food before the morning."

CHAPTER FORTY-SIX

Water dripped close by in an unending monotonous rhythm that echoed off dark but shiny stone walls and seemed to fall into step with the racing beat of Melody's heart like an accompaniment; one drip, two beats, one drip, two beats.

No searing pain stabbed at her forehead when she opened her eyes. Yet the deep shadows that held the light at bay turned her around in dizzying waves of nausea as she fought to sit upright. But with no visual reference, the best she could do was allow her mind to decide.

She slumped to the floor again with her head in her hands.

Beside her, fixed to the cold, stone wall by four rusty bolts, was a tarnished surface, an iron bracket and a thick chain. Her heart dropped. Sensing the inevitable, she grabbed the chain in the dark and ran her hands along its coarse surface until she felt the tug on her leg.

She dropped the excess chain to the stone floor, leaned back against the wall and ran her hands through her hair, realising then that her earpiece was missing. She searched the floor around her, wondering all the while if she had dropped it, or if her assailant had removed it, knowing that Reg and Fingers could hear her plight. There was no sign of the device on the floor or in her clothing, and once more, the reality of her situation found a fresh wound to dig its claws.

A slice of dim light shone from one corner. At least fifteen feet high, its dismal effect on Melody's prison reached the floor with enough power to light the fur of a rat, but not enough to illuminate a door.

Five steps in each direction were the limit of the chain, with each adjoining wall being six of Melody's steps from the iron bracket. She stretched to allow the trickling water to run across her fingertips then wet her lips. At the limit of the chain, she checked every possible inch of each wall. But she found no door and no window.

She resorted to scrambling on the floor for a trapdoor, but all she found was dirt, small animal bones and the droppings of the rats that circled the edges of the cell, sensing that feeding time had come. Infrequent chirps and squeaks from the rats were the only accompaniment to the incessant teasing of the water.

Having ruled out each of the walls as the exit, and having examined as much of the floor as she could, Melody leaned back and stared up at the light. There was a hole, three feet wide and as tall as a man, but there were no steps.

"It's an oubliette," she said to herself, hearing her whisper die in the damp, stale air. "I must be in the castle."

The stone walls and floor, and the ancient smell of years of debauchery, suffering and neglect that seemed to cling to the walls, all supported her theory. But nothing helped her escape. The only clue to her future lay in the bones of dead animals.

Once more, she examined the ankle cuff,

fumbling in the dark to understand the ancient mechanism. But with no tools and no light, it was guesswork at best. She considered using animal bones to work the lock, but there was no keyhole that she could feel.

As a last resort, Melody got to her feet, wrapped the chain around her hands and, by snapping the chain tight, tried to work the bracket loose.

She stopped after two minutes, having come to the conclusion that in the few hundred years the castle had been there, she would not have been the first person to try this technique. The exertion and the chloroform combined in a dizzying rush of poisoned blood to her head and sent her to her knees. Burning waves of nausea washed over her, forming a layer of cool sweat on her brow and nape until she lay flat on the cool floor.

A rat, emboldened by Melody's stillness tested the sole of her boot with three tugs. A swift kick sent it scurrying to the safety of the wall opposite, but more ventured in, each of them with their beady eyes set on Melody's body. She allowed the small pack to get close. Six small shapes darker than the floor twitched at her feet and legs. But only when they had all crept close did Melody attack, fighting them off with frantic violent kicks. She connected with one, and as it recovered from slamming into the wall, she stood up and stepped on its head, feeling the tiny skull crush beneath her foot.

She picked it up by its tail, and threw it to the far side of the room, then listened to the pack venture over and begin their meal. The reprise in their attack gave Melody time to think. But the dark walls and shadow induced no useful thoughts. She was sitting with her legs drawn up to her chin, cradled her head between her knees and wrapped her arms around her ankles.

Sleep came in fitful bursts. Undisturbed by the rats, her mind took her on short trips to the past. In every dream, regardless how inaccurate the scene, Harvey was by her side. Each time she woke, she checked for rats. But they were busy eating the remains of their friend. Then she checked the dim slither of light up high in the corner. But each time there was no change.

Until the last time she woke.

In the overwhelming darkness, she sensed more than saw, darker and heavier than the walls of her cell, the unmistakable shape of a man standing over her.

CHAPTER FORTY-SEVEN

The castle had long since lost its menacing drawbridge and portcullis. The moat was home to wildflowers that were rooted deep in the rocky ground, and high on the walls above potted trees hung from the walkways in the place of cannons and soldiers.

The entrance welcomed visitors with ornate carvings on two huge front doors that filled a giant archway. A symbol of what looked like two crossed swords had been carved into the keystone. But years of weathering had reduced the image to two unnatural grooves, wider than the natural cracks that adorned the old stone walls.

Where once there may have been torches

sitting in iron brackets to light the impressive hallway, electric lights had been fitted. Although sympathetic in design to the origins of the castle, they stole a slice of the medieval feel that manifested in the castle's very core.

The rug beneath Lola's feet stretched the length of the hallway, guiding visitors to two more doors, which Dumas opened and was standing beside, while waiting for her to help her father through them. The walls were home to old oil paintings, none of which Lola recognised as revered artists. But they were of impeccable quality nonetheless.

Each frame had been hung with precision and taste, equally spaced between the uprights so that each portrait was equally lit on either side. Dumas waited with a devilish smile on his face as if all his dreams had come true. He was standing beside an area of original bare stonework, cold to the eyes and out of place.

Dumas followed Lola's eyes and his smile weakened.

"One day," he said.

Lola stopped with her father and stared up at the space.

"Imagine how impressive it would look

there," Dumas continued. "It's almost as if it was meant to be."

"You'll never get it," said Smokey. "Not in our lifetime. The Guildhall Gallery was built around it. All the gold in the world couldn't convince the Society for the Protection of Sacred Arts to give it up."

"Not while the director is alive," said Dumas. "But who knows? Maybe the society would benefit from some fresh blood."

"And stolen gold?" said Lola.

"The gold belongs to me," he snapped. "It was stolen, and all you did was steal it back for me."

"Is that why we're here?" asked Lola. "I mean, I'm grateful for the tour, but if all you want to do is boast about your new found wealth, I'm sure there are other sights to see."

"I think we both know why you're here." Dumas spoke softly, his voice twinged with a sadness that even his arrogance could not belie. "Follow me," he said, then turned and disappeared through the doors. "And don't think about running. I'm sure even I can catch a one-legged man and his bitch daughter."

"Do you think Melody followed us?" whispered Lola.

"Of course. Don't worry, dear. Reg and Fingers will be watching this place from above, and Melody is probably scaling the walls as we speak."

They followed Dumas through the double doors and entered into a large room that had been decorated in a similar way to the hallway. Eight large windows cast eight bright shafts of sunlight onto the floor. A dining table was positioned at one end of the room in the shadow of a huge, dark oil painting. At the other end, two red, leather couches were positioned opposite each other with an ornate wooden coffee table placed in the middle. No paintings adorned the walls, just two simple and original torch holders from which hung chains and shackles. A pair of jewel encrusted daggers were mounted on the wall to one side.

"Do you know what those are for?" asked Dumas gesturing at the chains and shackles.

Lola didn't reply.

"When a man offended the Don of the castle, he would be stripped and hung there, humiliated until the Don grew bored or until he was replaced by another offender."

"And then he'd be killed?" asked Lola.

"No," her father cut in. "He'd be cast into the oubliette and left to die."

"What's an oubliette?"

Smokey and Dumas shared a moment of respect for each other's knowledge with a glance.

"It's French," said Dumas. "It's somewhere you put someone to forget them."

"To die?" asked Lola.

"To die," confirmed Dumas.

Lola tore her eyes from the chains and continued to take in the room.

On the coffee table was a silver tray. It was rectangular in shape with solid, gold-coloured handles at either end and finished with ornate patterns that ran across its surface. Three coffee cups had been placed on the tray along with a pot of fresh coffee.

It was only when Lola saw the pot that she smelled the coffee. The smell seemed to accentuate and complement the musky odour of the ancient room.

"I haven't finished in here yet," said Dumas. He appeared to have calmed down from his little outburst, and had returned to his boastful character. "I have great plans for this room."

Through a window beside the couches, Prosperity could be seen in the shallow cove.

"I'm sure you'll be very happy here, Dante," said Lola.

"Sit, please." Dumas offered them both a couch, took a seat himself and began to pour coffee. "We may as well be civilised."

Lola helped her father to one end of the couch, then took her place beside him. Her eyes darted across the room, taking in the small decorative flourishes that, at a glance, could easily be missed.

Central to the dining table, mounted with prominence, was the large oil painting framed in heavy brass. The painting depicted the Spanish army fleeing Gibraltar following their failed attack on the British. In the foreground, a Spaniard lay dying and refusing help from the English officers who were beside him.

"Don Jose de Barboza. It's about dying with honour," said Dumas. "Fascinating, isn't it? But we're not here to talk about my collection or my castle, are we? No? In that case, let's talk about why you're both here."

Both Lola and Smokey remained silent, choosing to see where Dumas led the conversation. Dumas placed his hat on the coffee table, ran his fingers through his silvery hair, and then leaned forwards to sip at his coffee.

"I'll start then, shall I? You've come to stop me and to get the gold. Maybe you'll return it. Maybe you won't."

"You're wrong," said Lola.

"Am I? So enlighten me."

The pause as Lola searched for the words was too long. Dumas read between the lines.

"So you've come to kill me? You see, I can't help but notice how pale you are, Smokey. How weak you've become. You've been bedridden for some time, I know, and confined to your wheelchair, which must have been dreadful for you. So you thought that coming here would draw me out of hiding. But as you can see, Smokey, I am not hiding."

"What makes you think-" began Lola. But Dumas raised his hand to stop her.

"The time for little girls to give their opinion is over, Lola. It is time for the adults to talk."

He snapped his fingers over his head and, from nowhere, a hand reached out from behind the couch and smothered Lola's face with a white cloth laced with chemicals.

Lola fought back. She kicked out, sending

the table across the room and the coffee to the floor. But the man was strong and the chemicals were powerful. The fight drained from her like blood from a wound. She felt her father beside her, defending her with his crutch. But her vision faded to black, and dreams of Spanish soldiers fleeing Gibraltar on the burning batteries, while the English sent cannon fire over their heads, filled her mind. The scene played over and over, looping time and again. And then nothing but darkness.

CHAPTER FORTY-EIGHT

"So how are you going to do it?" asked Smokey. The words of her father were the first Lola heard when consciousness found its way back to her. "I don't want Lola to see."

At first, the words formed part of a dream. They were a strange narration to an even stranger story where men on horseback appeared through the cannon smoke and formed a circle around Lola, who had been tied to a post.

"But she should see, Smokey. It will be a lesson to her. To watch her father die because of his actions will be her greatest lesson. And one, I'm sure, she'll never forget."

Men on horseback faded, replaced by

stone walls, paintings and two old men who were sitting opposite each other on red, leather couches. She gagged as she bit down on the cloth that had been tied around her head. A dull ache ran through her arms and hard steel restraints dug into her wrists with chains that were fixed to the wrought iron brackets where, a long time ago, those who had offended the Don were chained and humiliated before being cast into the oubliette to die.

"How," continued Dumas, "is your choice. To fall from these walls onto the rocks below would be quick and certain, but would leave little of you for Lola to take home. I know that's something you're keen on."

"You're sick, Dante. I thought after all these years, you'd allow me the decency of an honourable death."

"But do you deserve honour, Smokey?" said Dumas. "It will be by your own hand that you die, not mine. There's no honour in suicide."

Dumas leaned forwards and placed a small white tablet on the silver tray. Then he reclined back, crossed one leg over the other, and waited for Smokey to speak.

"'This is my alternative?" asked Smokey.

"You always were a smart man, Smokey. But don't be fooled by its appearance. Taking the pill will allow Lola here to mourn your body. It'll give her something to carry home and bury in those fine gardens of yours. But your death will be slow. The chemicals inside that pill will enter your bloodstream, sending its fire coursing through your body and eating its way through each one of your organs. The manner of your death will depend on which organ gives up first. You will suffer incredible internal bleeding and a pain unfathomed even by medieval standards. And, of course, Lola there will be watching, helpless while you squirm on the floor trying to rip your skin off to get to the source of the pain."

Lola gave a muffled outburst, incomprehensible even to herself.

"Ah, she's awake," said Dumas, standing to admire her with roaming eyes. "I apologise for your discomfort, Lola. But I didn't want you to miss the show. I understand that plans have already been made. You're rich, Lola. What will you do with all that wealth?"

Lola fought against her restraints, but her efforts were futile. She inhaled through her nose and felt her eyes wide with anger but wet with helpless tears.

"How do I know she'll be okay?" asked Smokey. "How do I know you'll let her go?"

"Oh, I won't be letting her go," said Dumas, his eyes fixed on Lola's. "She'll be my first mate, at least until she's proved to be trustworthy enough. Then perhaps I'll find some corner of the world to set her free. I have no argument with Lola."

He spun on his heels to face Smokey, who was staring at the pill.

"So what will it be, Smokey? The easy way or the hard way?"

"And what if I said neither?" said Smokey. The strength had gone from his voice, leaving behind the cracked and broken remnants of a once powerful man.

"That's easy," replied Dumas. "I'll force feed Lola the pill and it'll be you who will watch your daughter die. It will be a very slow and painful death. It's an easy choice you are faced with I'm sure, Smokey."

With all reasoning gone, Lola snatched at the chains that held her against the wall. She screamed within the confines of her gag. But all her efforts did were raise a smile on Dumas' face and cause her father to crumble further.

Smokey reached forwards and took hold of the pill, staring at it in the palm of his hand with the curiosity of a child observing a captured poisonous insect before it sank its teeth into his soft skin.

It was with clear regret that her father tore his eyes from the pill and stared up at Lola.

"Close your eyes," he said.

She wanted to scream at him, to tell him no, to wait for Melody. But his eyes told her that it was too late. He nodded once with his lips pursed and his face gaunt as he fought to hold himself together. For her sake.

"Do it," he said.

A tear rolled from his eye, but he didn't wipe it away or hide his face. For the first time that Lola could remember, her father allowed his emotions to run free. It was written in his eyes, in his face, in his slumped posture.

"Do it now, Smokey," shouted Dumas, sensing the tension between father and daughter. "Or it's the high jump for you. I'll throw you off myself if I have to."

Lola held her father's sorrowful gaze one

last time. In her mind and heart, she spoke volumes, telling him everything she should have said before. She told him how sorry she was, how he was a good father, but most of all, how much she loved him. She left him with a look that conveyed her open and broken heart.

The edges of her father's mouth curled briefly, revealing the faintest of smiles as if he'd understood everything from his daughter's look.

"Do it," screamed Dumas.

Her father nodded at Lola, who closed her eyes, letting the flood of hot tears that she'd fought so hard to hold back cascade across her skin. The urge to open her eyes and scream at her father was overwhelming. But to see him die in pain at his own hand was not the last image she would hold in her heart. Her mind scrambled to find an image of him to adore, to cherish. Anything but the shell of a man who was sitting ten feet away with a fatal pill in his hand.

The room fell silent.

Lola squeezed her eyes closed, searching for the sound of her dying father fighting the pain of his organs being eaten away by chemicals. But when the noise came, she abhorred the thud of her father's body hitting the stone floor, the sound of his struggles against the sparse antique furniture, and his final dying breaths. There were two loud thuds followed by a wild scream.

Then the room fell silent.

Lola's heart thumped. Her breath came in short irregular waves leaving her breathless. Images of what might confront her played across her mind, but her eyes would not open. Before she had fought to squeeze them closed; now she fought to open them.

Just a crack.

A slice of blurred light magnified by tears.

A little more.

A dark shape, familiar yet fearful.

She forced them open, blinking away the tears.

Harvey Stone.

CHAPTER FORTY-NINE

A scream echoed off the cold, stone walls, shrill and sharp in the thick, stale air. But just like the dim light, the noise had faded to a haunting whisper by the time it entered Melody's oubliette.

"Sounds like the fun has started without us," said Samuel, his perfect English articulated with its usual clarity. "We can have some fun of our own."

"Samuel?" she said. "What are you doing here? Help me get these chains off."

"I think we both know that's not going to happen, Melody."

The truth struck her like a brick to the head.

"You snake. Of all the people I thought-"

"You thought wrong."

"Why? At least tell me why."

"I thought that would be obvious. Dante is a winner. Smokey was destined to lose."

"With you by his side, he was bound to lose, Samuel."

Samuel laughed and paced away from her, his dark shape succumbing to the shadows until only his voice gave away his whereabouts.

"How long has it been? When did Dumas buy you?"

"Oh, a long time ago," said Samuel. "Years, in fact. It was perfect. I sent Smokey chasing shadows all across the country while Dante made us rich. In the meantime, I enjoyed the fruits of Smokey's labour."

"So this was planned?" asked Melody.

"No, but plans change. To be a winner, you need to roll with the punches, Melody. We knew Smokey would go after the painting. We knew he would try and stop us."

"You didn't count on me."

"And look how that worked out."

Melody searched the darkness for his

shape, but her eyes landed on the ladder he'd used to climb down into the oubliette.

A chance.

"What's happening up there?" she asked.

"Death."

He spat the word as if verbalising it had left a bad taste in his mouth. He let it hang in the air, clear and sustained with his breath.

"And me?" asked Melody.

Even Samuel's smile was audible. He inhaled, long and slow.

"Life," he said, but cut the word short. "If this is what you call living."

"With the rats? That's not my style, Samuel."

His face appeared beside hers, close enough that she could feel his breath on her skin.

"Like I said, Melody, to be a winner, you need to roll with the punches. How comfortable your life is all depends on how well you adapt to your new life."

She felt his finger brush her forehead, cold to the touch, yet soft like a lover. Melody braced herself against the wall. Her back became rigid with anger and fear, the muscles taught and hard. Her senses woke with pulsing stabs at his smell, his shape and his presence.

Samuel's finger traced the outline of Melody's forehead, sweeping the loose hairs to one side. He moved closer to crouch before her. The softest light from above lit the side of his profile to reveal a handsome man. But his dark, cruel eyes sunk into the shadow, allowing only a glint of light to shine through.

He blinked once, then let his finger trace Melody's nose. He let it fall to her lips then traced the outline of her mouth. Then it was gone. His hand hovered in front of her, teasing her, then dropped to her chest, removed of any tenderness. In the darkness, his breathing grew in intensity as he felt his way to excitement, leaving Melody clenched and waiting for her chance. Waiting for him to commit.

But instead he moved away.

He stepped back into the shadows.

"Are you going to play nicely?"

CHAPTER FIFTY

Three feet in front of where Lola was fixed to the wall, Harvey stared back at her. But it wasn't with the cruel, hard eyes she'd seen before. He had a look of compassion and for the first time, Lola attributed the man with human emotion.

There was a choking sound from behind him. Her father was on his front. Mucus hung from his mouth to the floor in a long, pink string. The only occasional jolt of life came as the chemicals broke through another part of his insides and teased a nerve with its acidic touch.

Any remaining strength washed from Lola's body at the sight of her father fighting for his last breath. Her legs buckled and the chains rattled against the stone as they caught her weight and buried into her flesh. But she felt no pain. The man who had raised her, who had taught her everything she knew and who had allowed her free rein to become who she was, was lying in a pool of his own vomit and blood.

It was not the memory she would treasure. But she feared it would be an image that would come to haunt her.

Beside her father, on the other side of the coffee table, Dumas stared down at his hands, which had been laid flat on the table's surface and pinned with the two long daggers that had hung on the wall in the hallway. His face was twisted in a blend of agony and anger as he sucked air through his gritted teeth and cursed in a long string of incomprehensible Spanish.

"There was nothing I could do," said Harvey.

Lola averted her gaze, letting her eyes roam the room for a mental distraction, fighting the urge to scream and shout and let the tears flow.

But Harvey's presence lured her back.

"You might want to close your eyes again," said Harvey.

A transformation took place in front of her. His eyes glazed over, returning once more to the cold hard stare that Lola recognised. A chill ran the length of her spine as Harvey turned away to stand behind Dumas.

Lola looked on with incredulity at Harvey's calm composure. He rolled his head from side to side, feeling the click at each extreme. Every part of her wanted Harvey to end Dumas, to make him suffer. The fight inside her was back, and her feet found the floor. Like a wild animal, she tore at the chains.

But Harvey remained calm. His control somehow overshadowed Lola's physical desire to tear Dumas apart.

"You want the gold?" said Dumas, striving to turn his head to see Harvey, but restrained by his pinned hands. "I'll give you gold. How much do you want?"

"You can't give me what I want," replied Harvey. "All you can do is ease the pain."

"What are you doing?" said Dumas. The authority his voice had carried just five minutes before had been replaced by a high-pitched childlike tone, full of fear and emotion.

Quiet as can be, Harvey stepped away and began to browse the wall decorations.

Lola screamed against the gag for him to kill Dumas who, seeing Harvey's back was turned, fought against the knives that pinned him down.

But Lola's plight went unanswered. And Dumas' hands remained fastened to the table.

A pair of pikes, six feet long, lay crossed above a wooden shield that bore the same cross-swords symbol as the keystone above the two front doors of the castle. A fine sword, sheathed in leather and decorated with animal bone, took pride of place between two of the huge windows.

But it was a mace that caught Harvey's attention, a ball of sharp iron spikes fixed to an eight-inch handle by a chain three-feet long. It would have taken a strong man to wield the weapon in combat. But the damage it would have caused as he swung the ball on the battlefield in deadly arcs would have been phenomenal.

With little effort, Harvey lifted it from its iron hook. He swung the ball back and forth, gauging its weight as he made his way to stand in front of Dumas.

Dumas' eyes rocked back and forth with the pendulum motion of the mace. He pulled against the knives. His body juddered as nerve endings tore against the ancient blades.

"What?" he said. "Anything you want. We all have a price. Just name it, and it's yours."

Without warning, Harvey swung the mace high over his head and slammed the spiked ball down onto the fingers of Dumas' right hand. Dumas dropped to his knees, growling in pain and letting his forehead rest on the table as if he was praying. Three of his crushed digits hung from his hand by thin strands of sinew. Shards of broken bone pro-truded from his skin and blood pooled into the deep grooves in the wood made by the sharp spikes.

Harvey raised the mace once more. The movement made Dumas too frightened to look up.

"I'm sorry," said Dumas, cowering his head into his shoulder. "He had it coming. If you only knew the things he'd done."

Harvey lowered the mace and peered over his shoulder at the corpse of Lola's father lying on the floor behind him. Blood had leaked from the old man's mouth and found channels in the old flagstone floor.

Bringing the mace high above him, Harvey forced the ball and chain to the table, destroying Dumas' other hand.

"It's not the first time I've removed someone's hand, Dumas," said Harvey. "I know what's going through your mind."

But Dumas was incapable of replying. Instead, a whimper of sound emerged from the back of his throat. He bit into his own arm as if he was restraining an outburst. But his agony was clear.

Lola savoured the moment. A run of saliva hung from her lips like a crazed savage, steering Harvey with evil thoughts of brutality.

"I know the torment," continued Harvey. "Hands are a crucial part of our existence. Without them, we're useless. There's a part of your brain now adjusting to that. It's thinking of all the things you can no longer do without help."

At the sound of Harvey's words, Dumas' face dropped. The fight had vanished.

"You're powerless, Dante. Everything

you've worked for, the power you fought so hard to obtain, it's gone."

Harvey took slow purposeful steps while he spoke. It was as if he was immune to Lola's thoughts. But when he turned and walked towards Dumas, her heart began to race once again.

"But another part of your mind can see past your ruined fingers and hands, can't it?"

With a violent snatch, Harvey grabbed a handful of Dumas' hair and wrenched his head back. Leaving the mace to fall to the floor, Harvey then picked up a ruined finger. He twisted it around, ripping what skin and sinew remained until it was free. An inanimate object held in front of Dumas' face. Tantalising but useless. Until it was forced into Dumas' mouth. Harvey held the man's mouth closed as he squirmed and tried to spit and stop the inevitable, involuntary swallow.

And then it happened.

Dumas convulsed, dry heaving as his own ruined forefinger made its way down his gullet.

"Was that the finger that pushed the button?" asked Harvey. "Tell me. Was it that finger? Or was it this one?" He picked up another and forced it into Dumas' mouth. The swallow came a lot faster than the first. Dumas shook his head to remove the bitter taste of irony blood and flesh, then spat blood to the floor, panting.

"What button?" said Dumas, once he'd caught his breath.

Harvey collected the mace from the floor and rose up high behind Dumas, ready to deliver the final blow to Dumas' head.

Lola watched, willing him with muffled pleas.

"The van," said Harvey. "You know what I'm talking about."

An understanding seemed to iron the agonised creases from Dumas' face. A smile grew, faint at first, but as the realisation dawned on Dumas, his head fell back, his body tensed, and a laugh, cruel and sickening, bellowed from the pit of his twisted stomach.

"The girl?" said Dumas. "It's the girl."

Harvey raised the mace.

But Dumas continued to laugh, fighting himself for a chance to speak and breath.

"You mean the little bitch who died in the blast?"

Two clicks of Harvey's neck, one to each side.

"The little tart you carried away from the museum? That's right, Harvey Stone, I saw you. I watched it all."

Harvey didn't reply.

"I told you before that I can give you anything you want."

"You can't give me what I want. You took her from me," said Harvey. He tensed his body in a powerful curve, gripping the mace with two hands over his head, and sucked in a deep breath, ready to smash Dumas' skull apart with a single blow.

Lola was frozen, torn between horror and delight. Her hot, gagged breath and endless tears had swollen and reddened her face. Her shackles had ripped her skin apart, leaving blood to run freely down her arms. But at that moment, she was free, flying high above the scene like a vulture relishing in the brutal act of life and death.

Dumas laughed once more, then cut it off in one short, sharp stab of laughter that caught Harvey's attention.

"She isn't dead, you fool."

CHAPTER FIFTY-ONE

With her back against the wall and the slack chain in her hand, Melody rose into a defensive posture. She held the chain behind her, ready to whip out at Samuel if and when he showed himself. Her head darted from left to right, seeking the shadows for subtle changes. But there was no sign of him. She strived to hear his polished brogues on the dirty floor, but her short breaths were loud in the tiny oubliette.

"You want me?" she said. "You come and get me."

A flash of hot breath against her skin to her right. Melody whipped the chain around;

it found nothing but the hard, stone wall and clattered to the floor. Rats scurried to the corner, squealing at the excitement as she dragged the chain back and prepared herself for another attack.

"You're scared," said Samuel.

But Melody couldn't place his voice. The rats, her pulse and her breath filled the room with an incessant hum.

"You should be," he whispered, just inches from her ear, sending her reeling and backing away as far as the chain would allow. But at the limit of the chain, there was no excess to use as a weapon. So Melody dropped it, closed her eyes and inhaled deeply to calm her breathing.

The squealing of the rats was a pitch high in the spectrum of sound. The dull thud of her heart in her ears with its bass tone was low. Although the walls to her sides were hidden by shadow, she pictured them in the light, as they once must have been, even for just a short time. Years of damp had stained the large stones with shades of greens and browns, and they glistened as an ever-moving layer of moisture flowed across them. The floor, bearing hundreds of years of dirt, grime and filth, was bare, save for the length of chain that held her captive.

The image formed in her mind clearly. Between the sounds of the rats and her heart was a void, in which tiny sounds took their place, pin pointing Samuel to the wall on her right.

Keeping her eyes closed, she stepped forwards. The chain dragged behind, metallic against the stone.

Samuel moved past her; the change in the air was apparent.

But Melody remained still. She pictured him walking around her, lustful thoughts stirring his loins.

Melody pictured breaking his neck.

She stepped forwards once more. Again, the chain dragged behind, forming a loop of excess, not quite enough to use as a weapon. But her position in the room was clear. He was behind her now, darker than the shadows, and hard as only a man can be.

Melody felt the temperature raise maybe half a degree. It was subtle, almost indiscernible, but it was there.

And then he was in front of her.

"Found you," he whispered.

His words brought only a smile to Melody's face. She had lured him close.

"Don't fight me," he said. It was as if he had only mouthed the words and allowed his breath to form the sound.

A long exhale was followed by a wandering hand, as it explored Melody's body with a tender, childlike touch. Samuel's breathing quickened. Though Melody kept her eyes closed, his rhythmic movements needed no explanation. The sounds of his torment grew in intensity with his groping hands and the waves of his stale breath on her neck as he leaned into her. He gave a final shudder and exhaled. His hard grip on her chest released, returning to his soft inquisitive touch, then he slid from her to the floor.

Her vision of the room became confused, a swirl of imagery. The walls were no longer on the sides. The rats were no longer behind her. Now a shadow loomed over her, as if its presence fed off the diminishing darkness to become greater than ever before.

She opened her eyes and dizzied at the

sudden intake of the dim light in the corner of the room, which framed a human form like the devil himself.

"Harvey."

CHAPTER FIFTY-TWO

The blade of the sword sucked at Samuel's flesh as Harvey pulled it from his body and hoisted Melody off her feet. Never before had he longed for a single kiss. Never before had he wanted Melody in his arms so much. Her legs wrapped around his waist, squeezing him tight. Her arms pulled him closer and her hands felt his face, his neck and chest as if searching for some flaw like she doubted it was really him.

They paused for breath with Melody held high, but neither spoke. There were no words. There was no light. Only two people, once lost and now found.

The kiss lasted an age, but not long

enough. When Melody relaxed her legs and slipped along his body to the ground, she still clung to him, running her hands across his chest.

"Do you know how long I've waited for that?" she asked, resting her head on his shoulder.

"Are you hurt?" he replied.

"Physically?"

Harvey didn't reply.

"Where's Dumas?" said Melody. The urgency returned with her senses.

"Smokey's dead."

"Was it-"

"Dumas?" Harvey interrupted. "Yes. I was too late."

"And he's here?"

Harvey nodded.

"I haven't finished with him yet."

The iron shackle on Melody's ankle was no match for the hard, steel blade, which prized the two halves apart and clanged to the floor beside Samuel's naked body. With a glance around the room, and seeing the dark form of the corpse, black against the charcoal floor, Harvey took Melody's hand and led her to the ladder. Once Harvey had climbed up behind her, he pulled the ladder up and tossed it to the floor.

"Is he dead?" asked Melody.

"He will be," replied Harvey. Then he took her hand again and made his way to the hallway, where he replaced the blood and filth stained sword to reform the wall-mounted cross.

Melody was already at the two wooden doors. She stopped to take in the scene with two slow movements of her head, then rushed inside. Harvey was standing at the entrance as Melody silently untied Lola.

Gasping for breath and erupting in tears, Lola fell onto her father's body, smothering him and willing him to reply, to move, to react in some way.

Harvey made his way over to the coffee table, where two sharp daggers remained, stuck in the bloodstained wood. Three fingers remained atop the table's surface, arranged like cutlery in a neat line, but crushed and destroyed.

Small chunks of flesh garnished the bloodied blades.

"Where is he?" asked Harvey.

But Lola had buried her head into

Smokey's chest, savouring the last time she would ever touch and feel her father's skin.

Melody looked from Harvey to the blades. Her eyes narrowed as she pieced the scene together and came to the right conclusion.

"Lola," she said, "where's Dumas? Where did he go?"

Sobbing, Lola raised her head and held Harvey's stare.

"He ran," she said. "He pulled himself free and ran, like the coward he is."

It was all Harvey needed to know. As Lola returned to grieve, Melody came to Harvey's side.

"We need to go after him," she whispered. "Do we leave her here?"

Harvey didn't reply.

He stepped away from Melody and opened the doors to the ancient battlement. A plant pot had been placed at one end, and a small table and chairs offered a view across the Mediterranean like no other.

"Melody," he called.

Then he waited to hear her boots on the flagstone floor. She sidled up beside him, working her way beneath his arm. Her body was warm in the cool, late afternoon air.

He pulled her closer to plant a kiss on the top of her head.

"Do you see that?" he asked.

"See what?"

"The view."

"I see it," she replied.

"Look closer."

Harvey followed Melody's eyes as they withdrew from the breathtaking horizon, across the glimmering shades of blue, and found Dumas' yacht moored in the bay.

A sudden intake of air told Harvey that she saw what he saw. Between the yacht and the dock at the foot of the cliffs, a tiny speeding dot made its way across the ocean, leaving a wake, white against the darkening water.

"Do you think that's where the gold is?" she asked.

Harvey didn't reply.

"We can't let him get-"

"Go and get Lola," said Harvey.

"No, Harvey. She doesn't need to see him get away."

"Do you trust me?" asked Harvey.

Melody hesitated, searching his eyes.

"With my life."

A soft kiss followed as if the words were not enough unaccompanied.

"Get Lola."

Melody loitered at the door, looked back, and then stepped inside.

"Reg, come back," said Harvey.

"Loud and clear, Harvey. It's good to hear your voice."

"Likewise, Reg. Sixty seconds."

"Copy that," came the reply, as Melody stepped through the doors with Lola in tow, her head lowered. She eyed Harvey with a shadow of distrust, but Melody shook her head, a subtle movement that seemed to ease Lola's fear.

"I want you to see something, Lola," said Harvey.

She looked up at him, but her mind was elsewhere.

"Sometimes, Lola, people take things from us. Things they can never return."

Harvey felt the sting of Melody's stare as she too listened to what he had to say.

"I know what you're feeling. I lost everything and I spent my life finding out why. It's why I am who I am. Believe me, Lola, I know you're hurting. I know it's hard. And I know that no matter how wrong it is, no matter how much you don't want to believe it, the only thing that will help you right now is revenge. The feeling will pass. No doubt, you'll be sickened by your own thoughts. But the thoughts will return. You'll always have this unsettling feeling in your stomach. A need to know."

"Harvey, stop," said Melody.

But Harvey didn't reply.

"I won't stop, Harvey," said Lola. Her voice was monotone.

She stared at him, and for the first time, Harvey saw no fear in her eyes, just the shine of her tears, and the swell of her pride.

"Come and stand beside me," said Harvey. He held her hand, and Melody moved across for her to stand between them.

"I want you to look out to that yacht," said Harvey.

Lola's breathing quickened. Her grip on Harvey's hand tightened, then relaxed.

"Prosperity," she said.

"Do you see him?" asked Harvey.

The grip on Harvey's hand tightened once more. Lola's chest rose and fell like the waves and troughs of an ocean storm.

"Use that, Lola. Feel it."

She stuttered an exhale, too violent to retain. Her eyes narrowed on the tiny dot that climbed from the boat into the yacht, helped by a younger man, slight in build and subservient even from afar.

Through Lola's clammy hand, Harvey felt her racing pulse, which matched her violent, rasping breath.

"Use it, Lola. Think of him. This is your one chance. Hold your father in your mind. Do you see him?"

Lola began to hyperventilate. Her swollen eyes bulged and she clung to Melody and Harvey, swaying with the power that coursed through her.

"I said do you see him, Lola?"

"Yes," she shouted.

"Louder, Lola. Do you see the man that killed your father? Can you see your father's face in your mind?"

"Yes," she called, then quietened. Her breathing slowed and a look of clarity washed across her tortured face.

Her eyes hadn't left the yacht once.

In the second of silence that followed, Harvey glanced across at her and smiled as a fireball erupted into the evening sky. The flames billowed, searching for oxygen and stretching with fiery fingers far across the water, then high into the air. A moment later, the dull thud of the explosion ricocheted off the castle walls. A black cloud of smoke mushroomed high into the sky, filling the small cove with black, fiery fog.

Fragments of Prosperity fluttered back into the ocean, diving and spinning in and out of the smoke that hung across the surface of the waves like a blanket. Lights from nearby boats flicked on one by one and swept across the water, searching the fog that had settled, and began to roll with the wind to reveal a final glimpse of the burning yacht. All that was left was a shard of white, brilliant against the darkening blue, as it slipped from sight and into the deep.

CHAPTER FIFTY-THREE

The service was held in Kent, God's Garden, as the signs by the roadside claimed. From there, the congregation moved to Smokey's estate for the celebration of life. On the grand terrace, hostesses in black dresses offered canapés and refreshments to guests, and a four-piece quartet lifted the spirits with the work of Pachelbel, Mozart and other tasteful compositions.

In attendance were members of various art organisations and politicians that were acquainted with Smokey with varying degrees of trust, like layers of an onion. The surface acquaintances, mostly politicians, provided anecdotal accounts of Smokey's projects, programmes and escapades in the hunt for the protection of art. The deeper layers of acquaintances, who had known Smokey when he was a struggling art thief, spoke loosely of his adventures with the tale focused on Smokey's passion for a particular painting.

The congregation was held on the grand terrace that overlooked the impeccable gardens. At the foot of the stone stairs, Harvey was standing looking out at the rows of hedges, the lake and the perfect lawns as the quartet entered into the opening bars of Samuel Barber's Adagio for Strings. A single haunting violin hung in the air with a single sustained note until, as if rising from the depths of sound, the remaining three emerged to support the lead.

Heads turned and the group parted as Melody cut a path through the congregation and stopped at the top of the stairs. She was dressed in a long, figure-hugging black dress and delicate black heels. A small, half-veiled hat was positioned with style at an angle that balanced the wave of fine hair she had allowed to hang from one side.

She held the balustrade as she descended the steps with an elegance Harvey had not seen in her before. A flash of light from her left hand caught Harvey's eye.

"You're not joining the party?" she asked, as she moved closer to him.

"I'm not the partying type."

"What type are you?"

"The type of guy that prefers quiet walks to idle chatter with strangers."

"Do you walk alone?"

"Sometimes, recently."

"Can I join you?"

Harvey didn't reply. Instead, he took Melody's hand and walked towards the bridge.

"You still wear the ring."

"I'm still engaged to be married, Harvey. Until somebody tells me otherwise."

Harvey didn't reply.

"So what are your plans?" asked Melody. "Do you still have the house in France?"

"Of course. Although I haven't been there for a few months. I've been a little occupied. I'll head back there for the winter."

They stopped on the stone bridge, which spanned the narrowest part of the brook that fed the lake.

"How about you? Do you still have the dog?" asked Harvey.

"Boon? Yes. Well, Reg and Jess have been taking care of him for the past few months. I've also been a little occupied."

"I actually miss that dog," said Harvey.

"I actually miss that house. I miss France, our beach, the garden."

She stopped, as if sensing that she was pressing too hard.

Harvey stood up straight, pulling Melody into him but holding her arms tight against her side.

He kissed her and let his hands slide up her bare arms, then across her shoulders to her neck, where his fingers traced the outline of her face. Harvey pulled away, letting his fingers wander across her lips.

"I miss us," said Melody.

Her white teeth bit into her lower lip in anticipation of his answer.

Harvey didn't reply.

The End

STONE FIST - SAMPLE
STONE FIST - BOOK TEN- CHAPTER ONE.

Sweat dripped from Fraser's swollen brow, it collected blood from the cut above his eye then fell to his knee where it ran down his leg and discoloured his white sock. In the one minute break between rounds, Fraser tried to control his heart rate, but all around him was a fear inducing blur of taunts, shouts, bright lights and abuse. Ahead of him, in the far corner, his opponent Mackie, was sitting, staring back at him while his trainer held a water bottle up for him to suck at.

"Let's go, boys," called the ref, a middle-aged man dressed in a white shirt and black trousers that struggled to contain his excessive paunch. "Round five."

There was no bell. The audience didn't fill an arena. The ring was in the basement of a pub in Plaistow where bare knuckle fighting provided high stakes for the every villain worth his salt for miles around. But the bare knuckle fights at the Golden Ring pub in Plaistow had one major difference; they were no holds barred fights to the death.

Plaistow was Fraser's home turf. Mackie was the guest fighter, but he was good and had got in early with the debilitating blow to Fraser's sight in round two.

"Get a move on," called someone from the crowd behind Mackie.

"Yeah get up and fight, you pussy," another shouted.

Mackie's red shorts were in the centre of the ring. Fraser could see them, rocking from side to side as his opponent bounced from foot to foot to kept warm and loose.

Fraser pushed off the ropes but held on for a second. His vision was returning, or so he thought. He turned his head from side to side trying to focus on something, anything. Movement in the corner of his eye caused him to duck instinctively and Mackie's arm swung across the top of Fraser's head grazing his shaved head. Fraser jabbed at him blind, felt the connection and followed through with a combination, the last of which glanced off Mackie's sweaty body sending Fraser stumbling forward.

That was when he knew it was over.

A hook out of nowhere connected with Fraser's head, he raised his arms to block the attack, but it was too late, the blows came fast, hard and with relentless brutality. Hard, gloveless, hammer-like punches that found their mark each time.

Three punches sealed the deal. The first to his temple slowed Fraser's world to a crawl, and the second to his nose brought with the familiar iron taste of his own blood; the third was an uppercut that shook the life from Fraser's mind and turned his world into a dance of swirling lights.

Then darkness as he hit the floor and felt the warm rush of adrenaline fighting a lost cause.

Spinning lights greeted Fraser when he woke. Angry shouts from the wild audience slowed and dropped an octave, as if someone had slowed time down.

"Finish him," yelled a man who had

climbed up onto the ropes and leaned into the ring, but all Fraser could see was a dark silhouette above him that seemed to turn as if Fraser was laying on a turntable. The man's voice was rough and hoarse from shouting but carried with it an authority. He wasn't just a member of the audience, he was Del Dixon, a renowned South London gangster who managed Mackie. "Mackie, get in there and finish it or I'll get in there and finish you myself."

More faces appeared at the ropes, keen to see the fight come to its ultimate conclusion.

Two knees dropped down onto Fraser's shoulders, slippery with sweat. The spinning slowed enough for Fraser to make out Mackie's blurred form.

For a moment the two fighters locked eyes, sharing some kind of kindred understanding.

Fraser understood what Mackie had to do. He was ready.

He nodded once and closed his eyes, before Mackie delivered his final blows. The first was a hook that turned Fraser's head to one side, ripping his neck muscle and breaking some teeth. But the pain was short-lived. The second blow crushed his Fraser's temple against the canvass floor of the ring, fracturing his skull. The third broke his jaw completely.

The fourth punch turned the lights out for Fraser but enough consciousness remained for him to hear the taunting, muffled count of five, six and seven, before Mackie's final punch opened Fraser's fractured skull and consciousness leaked away like bloodied water into a drain.

Also by J.D. Weston

Award-winning author and creator of Harvey Stone and Frankie Black, J.D.Weston was born in London, England, and after more than a decade in the Middle East, now enjoys a tranquil life in Lincolnshire with his wife.

The Harvey Stone series is the prequel series set ten years before The Stone Cold Thriller series.

With more than twenty novels to J.D. Weston's name, the Harvey Stone series is the result of many years of storytelling, and is his finest work to date. You can find more about J.D. Weston at www.jdweston.com.

Turn the page to see his other books.

The Silent Man

To find the killer, he must lose his mind...

See www.jdweston.com for details.

The Spider's Web

To catch the killer, he must become the fly...

See www.jdweston.com for details.

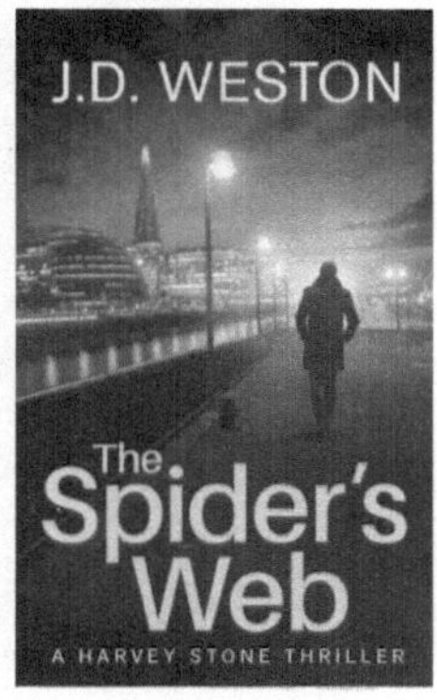

The Mercy Kill

To light the way, he must burn his past...

See www.jdweston.com for details.

The Savage Few

Coming 2021

Join the J.D. Weston Reader Group to stay up to date on new releases, receive discounts, and get three free eBooks.

See www.jdweston.com for details.

THE STONE COLD THRILLER SERIES

The Stone Cold Thriller Series

Stone Cold

Stone Fury

Stone Fall

Stone Rage

Stone Free

Stone Rush

Stone Game

Stone Raid

Stone Deep

Stone Fist

Stone Army

Stone Face

The Stone Cold Box Sets

Boxset One

Boxset Two

Boxset Three

Boxset Four

Visit www.jdweston.com for details.

The Frankie Black Files

Torn in Two

Her Only Hope

Black Blood

The Frankie Black Files Boxset

Visit www.jdweston.com for details.

A NOTE FROM THE AUTHOR

The Stone Cold Thriller series is, as you probably know by now, mostly set in London, where I worked for many years. In my early days I worked as a brick layer and then as an engineer and a pipe-fitter on many building sites across London. As such, I soon got to know many of the drinking holes across London that were tucked into narrow, cobbled side streets or boasting an outdoor seating area so we could sit and watch London in the summer time; purely to wash the dust from our throats you understand?

The City of London, with its perimeter security is steeped in history and grandeur and is one of the most protected cities I know of. So of course, there had to be a Stone Cold Thriller that faces that immense challenge, and that's where the idea for Stone Deep came along.

I hope you're enjoying the wild ride? And
I hope you're ready for some more...
Thank you for reading.

J.D.Weston

To learn more about J.D.Weston
www.jdweston.com
john@jdweston.com

ACKNOWLEDGMENTS

Authors are often portrayed as having very lonely work lives. There breeds a stereotypical image of reclusive authors talking only to their cat or dog and their editor, and living off cereal and brandy.

I beg to differ.

There is absolutely no way on the planet that this book could have been created to the standard it is without the help and support of Erica Bawden, Paul Weston, Danny Maguire, and Heather Draper. All of whom offered vital feedback during various drafts and supported me while I locked myself away and spoke to my imaginary dog, ate cereal and drank brandy.

The book was painstakingly edited by Ceri Savage, who continues to sit with me on Skype every week as we flesh out the series, and also throws in some amazing ideas.

To those named above, I am truly grateful.

J.D.Weston.